Praise for *What's Not Said*

In the venerable tradition of interlinking tales, *What's Not Said* conjures up with admirable cohesion a set of characters that scintillate with the feel of life as lived. Right from the beautiful opening paragraph, these stories display a deep sense of place and time, and their locally inflected articulacy describes, in a stirring irony, a world where territory, emotional as well as physical, seems always at stake. Sometimes tender and lonesome, the stories portray lives regulated by confusion and sudden violence, by a destruction that threatens from without and within. As one story has it, you can feel 'hell burn from deep inside it' alright, but this collection highlights above all else the imaginative joys to be found in the unflinching realist's eye.

– John Kenny
John McGahern Lecturer in Creative Writing, NUI Galway

Cursed land plots and scarred foundations. Shadow estates and blistered lives. Drug feuds and death alleys. Whether for blood, money or tears, actions speak loudest in Joyce's vividly unsettling landscapes. At some unspoken level, the cast members of these courageous, violent and yearning stories know, that from the get-go, they and those around them are being pushed off course. A very fine achievement.

– Alan McMonagle,
Author of Liar, Liar

What's Not Said

James Martyn Joyce

What's Not Said

What's Not Said

is published in 2012 by
ARLEN HOUSE
42 Grange Abbey Road
Baldoyle
Dublin 13
Ireland
Phone: +353 86 8207617
Email: arlenhouse@gmail.com
arlenhouse.blogspot.com

ISBN 978–1–85132–038–7, paperback
978–1–85132–048–6, hardback limited edition

International distribution by
SYRACUSE UNIVERSITY PRESS
621 Skytop Road, Suite 110
Syracuse, New York
USA 13244–5290
Phone: 315–443–5534/Fax: 315–443–5545
Email: supress@syr.edu
www.syracuseuniversitypress.syr.edu

Typesetting by Arlen House
Cover artwork 'Wearing Memoirs' by Dagmar Drabent
www.dagmardrabent.com
Cover design by Paul Callanan
www.designassociates.ie
Cover photography by Joe Geoghegan

Contents

ACKNOWLEDGEMENTS

What's Not Said grew out of a stroke of good fortune, my adoption by The Talking Stick Workshop in Galway: Geraldine Mills, Hedy Gibbons-Lynott, Siobhán Shine, Gerard Hanberry, Hugo Kelly and Alan McMonagle. Established writers in their own fields, they have given me the time and the air to tease these stories out, to focus and to give them light. I thank them for their support.

My gratitude to James C. Harrold, Galway City Arts Officer and to Galway City Council for an individual Artist's Grant (2011). Thanks also to the Tyrone Guthrie Centre at Annaghmakerrig where many of these stories were edited and rewritten.

My thanks to Dagmar Drabent, artist, for the original cover image, 'Wearing Memoirs', to Paul Callanan for his reworking of that image and to Joe Geoghegan, photographer for the author photograph.

Appreciation and thanks to Geraldine Mills, Alan McMonagle, Mike McCormack and Dr John Kenny, NUIG for their close reading of the manuscript and to Alan Hayes of Arlen House for his patience, his editing and his propensity for risk-taking.

Finally, though many of these stories are inspired by a particular place – Galway – all of the characters are fictional as are the scenarios and the exact locations.

Dustwoman was shortlisted for a Francis MacManus Award; *Angelground* was shortlisted for the William Trevor Short Story Competition; *Being Mister Smith* was shortlisted for The Trevor/Bowen Prize 2011.

James Martyn Joyce
Galway, 2012

dedicated to
transplant surgeons,
Mr Patrick I. Condon, Waterford
and Mr Sheraz M. Daya, London,
without whose expertise I would
have been unable to complete this book.

What's Not Said

Dustwoman

The evening my father had the brush with the dustwoman will always be with me. They were digging a grave over by the elm-tree wall, the town a haze in the distance, the little quilted farms patterned to the river, the narrow fields spreading away down to the low land with its boggy pools and twisted scrub, the wind light, the evening light.

There was my father Tim, with Big John and Mike, the usual crew. It was a young woman's grave, not that it mattered, but it was and it would be dishonest to say otherwise. They went down easily, not a first opening, the soil piling high on the old boards, the pebbles and the brown clay trickling, the fist-sized stones running back. Big John shifted the most as usual but it was my father who hit the timber.

That was the slang they used, 'hitting the timber', touching the coffin of the previous corpse buried there. The box was old but fairly solid, the lid still strong, the nameplate pitted with corrosion from the seeping rains and the heavy soil, no name that they could see, but should I say that was what prompted them to lift the lid? Who knows?

The last name on the stone said Judith Grey, aged nineteen, daughter of Henry and Olive who were buried there as well. He was shaking when he told us: my mother, Gran and me, how he'd braced his back, the shovel thrown aside, I can see it now, the blade-point worn to a sad, sickle mouth from years of digging, and Mike and Big John balanced on the lip urging him on.

'G'wan Tim, one good wrench will do it, she'll not bite you', Big John called and my father had spat on his clay-creased hands and caught the overlapping edge and pulled. Were they grave robbers? Technically I suppose.

She'd only lived for a few seconds, the dustwoman in the box. He'd ripped the lid back and there she was, preserved as the day she had been buried, her gold hair and pale-flesh face, her eyes closed and colour in her lips. Then, meeting with the air she was gone, her structure folding back, dust tears trickling down her dust cheeks, her brow peeling, her closed eyes gone, the lashes gone, the lids a fine dust, all falling back into her empty eye sockets, the air kissing her until only the skull and her sickle smile and her matt of golden hair remained. My father had cried out and scrambled from the grave, Big John's and Mike's helping grip swinging him clear.

In the end Big John had jumped down and kicked the lid back into place, the rictus smothered and they'd shovelled in a thin layer to bury the ripped timbers. Then they'd gone home all thoughts of the usual evening pints abandoned and now my father stood there telling my mother and his own mother how it had been. They forgot me there in the small dark, so I backed quietly below the table top, easing into the domain of old shoes, the slight clinging smell of socks, grey caterpillars of dust. He had stopped shaking by then but he knew he'd stepped into a new place, I can see that now, a new place and for him a sacred place, a place of definite violation.

Gran rocked gently in the big chair by the glowing range, her deck of prayer books wedged around her, each one used according to the feast day, or the day of the week, or even the time of the day.

'You're a lucky man Tim King', she said when she'd let him settle after a short silence. 'Very few men get to see a blessed vision such as you have. It'll bring you nothing but luck'. Then she'd prayed aloud and gone back to her gentle rocking, her left hand covering her left eye as she mumbled the prayers, moaning out her chants from the fat, black missal.

My father never mentioned the event after that and I was too young to talk of it to Big John or Mike on my trips to the graveyard in the evenings after school. We never spoke of it again but it was there always, just underground, a hermetic wraith in the earthy dark, something forever remaining unsaid.

I liked these visits to the graveyard, the angular, resting stones; the tall crosses, the silence, the unexpected new openings and the gentle mounds. I liked the way the people were different in the graveyard too, kneeling by their loved ones, brushing earth from the hewn slabs, dressing them with flowers or simply praying.

Sometimes I would find them talking, usually 'kneeling-back' as I called it, resting on their heels, a few plucked weeds or a bunch of withered stems by their left hand. They would talk to the person underground, telling them stories of the family, loved sisters or brothers, a son astray, a daughter in bad luck. And I would ease down quietly and listen, resting by some flat stone or tall cross, out of sight while they sighed or wept or chatted, my big fear that MacEoin the Cemetery would find me and have my ear in his rough pinch and march me to my father, his horse-breath coming in long hisses, his nostrils wide.

MacEoin the Cemetery was the caretaker; he was my father's boss and Big John's and Mike's too. He lived in the stone house set solid into the graveyard wall, its blindside to the town, its own walls part of the curtain wall, holding itself inside with the dead, its windows high and painted white, each small pane an eye etched in light, the eyes watching for movement and seeing none.

He'd lived there alone for years, a fixture, the longest living thing in the land of the dead but even that would change with time. One of the many changes coming as it did with Frayne, touching us all with a lingering touch.

'There's a new man on the job'. My father made the announcement one evening at the supper, my mother's hands in her apron by the pan, my grandmother in pride of place at the head of the table, chewing, her prayer books closed for food.

'Frayne, he's out from the town. He started Monday'.

My father said no more but we knew there would be more, his announcement setting Gran in motion, a long trail of Fraynes tracked until she managed to corner the family in question to a terraced house on Breech Street, discussing neighbours and possible relations until she delivered the golden seed that 'unless she was mistaken', this Frayne was related to MacEoin the Cemetery. He would be in line to inherit the stone house when the caretaker retired, my father's face darkening further with each new gem, his mother's looks confirming him, somehow, of his stupidity, his guilt in the whole affair.

How often have I wished, looking back, that it had worked out like that but no, instead, MacEoin had keeled over one day, blubber in the sun, his face blue, his neck bulging out over his buttoned collar, onto a half-cleaned horizontal slab, his breath coming in sucked gulps like some floundering fish, a slow trickle of spume wetting the mottled surface, the nineteen of the date of death embedding its shape in the flesh of his fat cheek.

The ambulance carried him away to a long-term bed in the hospital, his job dropped into limbo until he lived or died. As the senior man, my father was moved into the stone house as acting caretaker, Gran sniffing at the excesses and decays of MacEoin's singular existence, the rows of worn-out boots in the back scullery, their soles hacked through and scarred from the digging, their uppers twisted from wet and wear, the selection of overalls holed below the waterline, hanging on nails like discarded pelts, a denied reluctance to dispose of them their only saving grace.

'Not much cleaning done around here', Gran announced, running her finger along the surfaces, her arthritic knuckle rigid with superiority and my mother set to putting the lot to rights, a flurry of dusting until the house felt fresh, felt like it was ours, as it did with time.

In time too O'Kane from the Council came out, a soulless smile worrying his thin lips, a single sheet of white paper in his hand. He put my father in the picture; he would be the acting caretaker, the senior man, until MacEoin returned, retired or passed away at which time the job would be advertised. My father nodded, he knew there was a reckoning to come, he held O'Kane's even stare, Frayne barrowing soil by the elm-tree wall, O'Kane following his slow progress.

'Keep things right Mister King, keep things right', O'Kane smiled. 'You're on the inside track', and he closed the thin satchel, the single sheet of paper safely buried inside.

And that was how it was. We moved everything then from Gran's little place into the stone house and the time behind the curtain wall became my home. We moved from room to room, Gran still grumbling, our eyes round, wondering at the space, the high ceilings, and the dark furniture. I would have my own room now once my father managed to move all of the empty packing cases and old papers out of the back storage space. My grandmother would have one too with my parents' room to the front, bigger than Gran's entire cottage and brighter too.

My father kept things right and a year, almost two slipped by, MacEoin the Cemetery a grey, kneaded lump in the hospital, my father his only visitor, bringing him the news of the most recent burials, the new plots opened, anyone who'd bought a double grave. Sometimes he spooned the mashed food into MacEoin's slack mouth, wiped the spit away and I would sit at the hospital window and watch the rooks blowing like charred leaves above the black woods, or the tall, thin daffodils struggle through another sudden shower.

At the funeral my father was treated like MacEoin's brother, men pressing his hand in sympathy saying how MacEoin was lucky to have had someone like him, my father nodding, always nodding. Frayne stood by the head of the coffin with several recent relatives who had come out of the woodwork, his dark face set, his eyes playing on the crowds, his lips suitably moist.

The same men praising my father pressed close to Frayne too as they passed, a whispered word, a gripped arm, a proffered hand and Frayne would smile and nod, as if knowing something, agreement and acceptance coming easy to him.

As ever the waiting was the worst part, my mother scanning the local papers for the job advert. Almost six months passed and still nothing, Frayne's work rate rising to challenge my father's, the graves delicate with pruning and design, weeds driven underground, the paths clear and gravelled, a steady crunch under the mourners' feet.

And then, one day, O'Kane was there, a pinch of thin sheets removed from the worn satchel, a copy offered to all of the men, my father and Frayne the only takers.

My father's suit hung on a nail by the far wall of the stone yard, the breeze airing it, my mother gentle with the wet cloth, all the stains safely gone, her iron pressing pleats into the heavy serge. The interviews spread over Saturday, my father and Frayne and the others from outside all sitting on the long bench, the steel-grey secretary calling each in turn through the long, empty afternoon.

The letter, in brown, sat on the kitchen table, my grandmother praying over it like some exorcist priest, her bad eye covered, her good hand raised, her imploring prayers sandblasting the table surface, my mother staying busy in the yard. I ran to the farthest corner where my father and the men were digging a grave. I passed Frayne on the way, a wire brush and a bucket of heavy bleach by his knees. He was working on an old slab, picking lichen from the letters with a short blade.

'Hurry on now Robbie', he giggled as I passed. 'Tell your daddy the news', that odd smile playing around his eyes and he turned back to swill the bleach across the stone, a slight hiss on contact.

'There's a letter'. My father paused in his digging, his shoulder level with the graveside, Big John and Mike piling the soil high on the boards pretending not to hear.

I'll never forget his eyes, a craving and the haunted stare of knowing the answer before the question was put. His life not in his own control, like he would never climb out of that grave, that hole, unless the friendly hand was offered and Frayne had taken care of that.

'It's coming wet', was all he said. 'I'll be in when this is done', and he bent to his digging again, the worn mouth of the shovel scooping, and the flash of the steel. I turned away back along the gravelled path, the dull, heavy sound as the shovel hit the timber stopped me, but he never looked, never lifted.

The letter ran to two lines, he had not been successful in his application for the job of caretaker. We would be moving out of the stone house and into some council house in the western estates, at least O'Kane had found us that. He let it drift to the tabletop without comment, his eyes looking to the window, the heavy rain nailing the windowpanes, my grandmother's sighs rising to heaven as he lifted his heavy oilskins from the nail and pushed past my mother, his face averted, her arm brushing his sleeve, her face a broken frame, her eyes closing, the tears squeezed out and my grandmother's harsh curse after her when she ran from the room.

The crashes came, steady, numbered and alive. It was dark; I was awake and moving, the rain still clattering on the tiled roof, the wind whistling. The crash came again and my mother's voice faint above the din and my grandmother's crying too. I ran to my parents' bedroom at the front, the curtains open to the night, another crash, glass falling, and its tinkling cry. My father stood below me in the rain, staggering, his face a bloody mask, the long shovel in his upraised grip, my mother and his mother around him clinging, trying to hold him back as he smashed the small panes, the glass showering as he moved slowly around the stone house, all the small panes breaking, the delicate frames splintering, torn eye sockets, rain tears, the black sheen of his oilskins, the ripple of his shoulders as he swung, a run of light along the polished handle, the sickle grin of the shining blade.

Flushed Out

We were trapping rats around by the back wall of the army barracks, Jacky standing astride the large pipe, the constant flow of brown water holding him, his eyes on the gape of the opening, the mouth of it between his legs.

'Here it comes', he cried. 'Flushing time, here it comes!'

And Bartley waited, all frown and total quiet, his squinty eyes on the wire mesh of the two cages set firmly in the channel, a rock inside each to steady them, their ends propped open with a stick, the strings coiled like weeping veins around his dirty palm.

It was my job to hold the dogs on the short, thin twines and my glasses kept slipping. Captain was whimpering like he could feel them coming, his ears up, his eyes on the pipe, his feet a dance happening outside of himself as he stretched to break. Tweek just lay hunched on the flattened grass, the twine around her scrawny neck, the wind raising tears in all our eyes, a knife filleting us, building hearts in us. All of us were eleven and 'on the mitch' from school, without a watch between us, one ear cocked for the beating bell, the church telling us the time, home by three, it sang, home by three or there'll be trouble.

Jacky was dancing on the pipe now, listening for the flow, the after dinner flush we called it, five hundred soldiers on the hill above us, hitting the latrines, full of whatever the cooks had managed to throw together and we were watching for the water rats to come darting from the mouth ahead of the rushing wave.

Bartley was hoping that the slice of soggy pan would tempt one or maybe two rats into the mesh or the flow would wash them there, another couple of fighters for Saturday's baiting in his backyard. His brother was five years older and paying him for a supply of ready victims, setting Tweek on them, hissing her on, Tweek, in her heyday, snapping them like twigs, her paws like a guillotine, dropping, breaking their brittle backs.

'Here it comes, here it comes'. Jacky cried again and we could hear the familiar squeaking and even though we knew it well, it always sounded strange, the piercing chirps as the rats raced before the rush, the water warning them to get out, get out, Bartley's traps, open-mouthed waiting, Bartley hopeful that a few of them would see the bread or miss the sight of the wire cages altogether in their rush and he'd drop the gates like lightning, one pull, the sudden slap and no way out.

Captain was almost foaming now, his neck stretching the twine around my wrist, Tweek still flattened, her eyes diamond bright, nothing else moving, not even a twitch of eyebrow as the gush of water rats burst from the mouth. Jacky was dancing like Popeye in the pictures, the same manic cackle, and a cry of release as the water burst onto the ebb rocks, the cages deluged in it, all sight of them lost and Bartley sprung the strings, slapping them down. Jacky and himself dashed forward, ignoring the smell, the threat of waste, letting the water drop, watching as it burbled out leaving the crates askew, the heavy rock holding each one more or less in position.

'Three! Three!' Jacky was screaming. 'We got three! No! Six! Six! We got six!'

He jumped down off the pipe and helped Bartley to drop another stone to seal the mesh lids in place before the prisoners realised that they could still escape.

I eased forward with the two dogs, holding them tight on the twines, Captain dancing tall now, his tail a stiffened curve. Tweek was still almost silent, her eyes feasting on the squirming prisoners, a low growl in her throat. And we had done well, three fat, sleek water rats in each cage, this was treasure. They were all fully-grown, writhing over and through and around each other, their eyes blazing red, their coats an oily black as they pushed against the blocked gates, the stones holding, their squeaks driving Captain into vertical jumps of anxiety.

These were our Thursdays, not every Thursday because that would be a pattern but the ones when Old Olly was on the warpath, the homework lost or forgotten in a blaze of football, the evenings like long elastic stretching the length of our street.

We'd meet at the garage near the canal and slip the bags behind the fence and then we'd decide, west to the sea cliffs, or out along the railway line, trailing the tracks, skipping the sleepers, our ears ready for the rumble of a train, as far as the army barracks or sometimes even as far as the woods beyond that again.

Then Bartley's brother got a new pup, Tweek the Ratter, a little ball of hair and muscle, all snuffle and needle teeth, and he set to training her, following the shoreline hoping for rats but getting very few until Bartley, bright as always, hit on the idea of bringing the rats to Tweek and we became rat-catchers, waiting for the burst from the barracks pipe, our traps baited, the gates propped.

Everyone avoided the overflow pipe and its mixture of decaying food and waste, with its rats and vermin, the gulls calling above it, crying. But, again, Bartley knew where to look and we'd wait downwind, the morning stretching, our skimpy lunches long eaten, and the dogs raising birds from the briars and scrub trees below the barracks wall until Jacky would cry. 'Flushing Time!' and we'd rope the dogs and set the mesh cages, a sea rock to weigh them down, and take our chances.

And this was the best ever, six rats in all, the two cages squirming as we ran along the shoreline like black dots in a painting, the tide far out, the sun blinding us, the dogs dancing free, the cages dangling from the short wire handles until we were safely away from the outlet pipe and we turned down the narrow laneway by the bridge. We knew an old farmer lived there with his wife and family but he never bothered us, and Bartley set about transferring our prey into one cage, prodding their oily flanks with a stick, their teeth nipping it, Captain's whimpering frenzy exciting them even more.

Some weeks we'd get nothing at all and Bartley would hide the cages along the railway slope, covering them with scrub and furze and we'd dawdle back to join the freed legions at the school gates. Then we'd amble home, our bags collected, our friends jealous but admiring, warning us of getting caught, of the trouncings we'd all get.

But today we had six rats, Bartley transporting them in the larger cage, a struggling muscle-bunch of fur and eyes and teeth, he'd stash them behind the railway sheds and collect them later when we'd eaten and the soccer games started in the street.

'Watch for the praying grannies', Jacky called as we split up towards our houses, our schoolbags retrieved, our stories set, and the dogs nuzzling at our heels.

'Yeah'. Bartley nearly smiled. He'd almost been caught one evening in November, rounding into our street, the night suitably dark, a fat water rat caged when Old Mrs Quirke on her way to devotions at the church cried out of the darkness, 'Jesus, what's that in the box?' And then he'd seen the others; the other three grannies and he'd bolted. He told his mother later that it was 'Duck' Dooley's cat and how he'd found it, and brought it safely back home.

'Those ould bitches told my mother'. We were stretched out on the sloping edge above the sea, the barracks off to our right, the battlements still grey even in the sunlight, and the rattle of rifle fire as the soldiers pumped bullets into the buttes, the sand popping as they hit. We were watching a fat cargo ship muscle its way through the 'roads', the little pilot boat bobbing around it.

'Jesus, what would you have done, if they'd caught you?' Jacky's eyes were big as plates. 'If they'd really seen what you had?'

'Dunno, I'd have run, let the rat go. Don't know'. And Bartley squinted out to sea and Jacky shouted 'Flushing Time' and we went with the slope, tumbling forward, our legs almost leaving us behind, the dogs around our heels, tripping us too.

Would Bartley's brother pay us the usual? He'd paid for one and doubled it for two, but six? Our market had to be limited and Tweek was getting too good at killing, her teeth snapping them, never letting them nip her on the nose while we sat on the fence and cheered. Bartley's brother would goad her, his hisses setting her, before tipping the rat in and Tweek would sweep in and snap, her teeth razoring and Bartley's brother would go 'good dog' and rub her and sling the carcass into Cawley's hedge because no-one liked the Cawleys.

'You weren't at school today Robbie, were you?' The silence around the table as my mother and father looked straight at me, my little sister eating the pattern off her plate.

'I was. I was too'.

'No Robbie, you weren't, Dad met Old Olly this evening, remember he taught your father too'.

And that was it, I had to admit that I was 'out the line'. Then they squeezed Jacky and Bartley out of me, but they knew already, I could feel it. Someone had told them, they knew already and I could give a good guess who that was.

'The 'grannies' told you, didn't they?' I was angry at getting caught; those ould bitches were trouble for us all.

'No Robbie, and don't call them 'grannies', Mrs Quirke and her sister and the Cawleys are good women. They do a lot for the church and for old people'. I could feel the heat in my mother's voice; it was time to shut up.

I could see the football game from the bedroom window, the usual sweep of children, defence and attack, all the same surge, up and down but there was no sign of Bartley or Jacky so we'd all been told on. Who else could it be? Just ould bitches and not minding their own business.

We all agreed it had to be them the next day at school. It had to be them. We'd get even we all agreed again. Bartley said nothing but we thought his father had hit him, there was a dark bruise on his cheek, but his eyes were narrowed. He slipped off to collect the cage that evening on the way from school. It was risky, still bright but he covered it with his coat and made it back to his own backyard without meeting anyone.

Our football games were banned until Monday and Saturday would be tough, I would have to tidy the yard and stack the logs and do anything else my mother could think of and Bartley and Jacky would probably be doing the same.

I spent the following day sweeping our yard, Captain playful with the brush, worrying it, but I wasn't in the humour and he retreated to his box by the shed. About lunchtime my father appeared to check on my work. He was all business but I had done a good job, the wood stacked against the shed, all the empty coal bags folded and the full ones standing upright by the outside tap. I felt him watching me so I kept sweeping, dragging the dead leaves away from the kindling I'd chopped earlier. He moved around me, watching.

'The "grannies" have been to the priest'.

I'd never heard him refer to them like that before.

'Old Mrs Quirke says someone kicked her door yesterday evening and they smashed her flowerpots too'.

I couldn't look him in the eye so I kept sweeping.

'Was that you? Do you know anything about it?'

The drag of the bristles filled the silence.

'No Dad, I came straight home, I was with Jacky, ask him'.

'And Bartley?'

'We left him off first at his house'.

'That's near Cawley's and Quirke's too'.

'Yes, but Bartley wouldn't do it, he wouldn't, Dad'.

He looked straight at me.

'As long as you had nothing to do with it. Is that clear?'

'Yes Dad'.

And he turned to go but then he stopped.

'They didn't tell on you but do you know who did?'

I shook my head.

'Do you want to know?' He placed his hand on my shoulder and pointed.

'He did'.

'Who?'

'He did'. And he nodded towards Captain. 'He goes to school with you every morning and when you go in to your class he comes home and lies on the doorstep'.

'Yes, I know'.

'He never comes home the days you go 'mitching' because he goes with you, isn't that right?

'Yes Dad'. And I could see it then, how simple it was, how very plain and simple.

We waited in the laneway to 'Duck' Dooley's shed opposite the church; the three of us huddled against the biting cold wind blowing in from the bay. Bartley or Jacky hadn't been in school on Monday and they'd missed the evening soccer but they'd suddenly shown up just as the game was getting good and nodded me towards them. Bartley looked hungry and cold and his jaw was black, a yellow bruise below his left eye.

'Meet us at 'Duck' Dooley's lane at half eight, we have something to do'.

'What?' I could feel that blankness in my chest like when Old Olly picked me out for singing.

'Just a little fun', he nodded. 'And Robbie, leave the dog at home'.

'But ...'

'Leave the dog at home. And keep your mouth closed, ok?'

He was angry, I could see it, feel it even, like the day he had the fight with one of the Duignans and Bartley had torn into him, knees and teeth, Duignan's lips a bloody mush and we'd had to lift Bartley off him because we thought he'd kill him and Duignan was at least fourteen and big as well.

'Ok'.

So I'd played on, one eye on the church, knowing that the devotions started at eight and I'd have to guess it after that. I'd pushed Captain through our back gate and sprung the latch, his scratching loud as I hurried away, and here we were shivering by the lane wall, Bartley leaning, with his shoulder against it, his eyes fixed on the church.

I wanted to say something about what had happened, but where would I start? Both of them looked angry, Jacky stubbing his toe on a stone at the base of the wall.

'What are we going to do?'

They both looked directly at me and Jacky laughed.

'We're going to lift those ould bitches out of it. Someone told our parents and they need a lesson'.

I wanted to tell them, I wanted to, but Bartley looked so shut in, chewing his knuckles like he'd been in a fight. So we'd give them a fright, jump out shouting and they'd scream and we'd run home in the dark and who'd know it was us? No one, yes, no one.

Bartley never turned, never took his eyes from the church and then the big arched door opened and the first of the people started to come out.

'Wait'. He still didn't turn, Jacky peering over his shoulder. I could hear the hum of the people chatting as they parted, ones and twos leaning off in different directions.

'Wait'. He was watching for some sign. I could hear my heart. I was hoping we'd jump out and scare them, which would be fun. Lift them off the ground with fear and run, our lungs bursting and our laughter carrying us all the happy way home.

'OK, they're coming'. And Bartley turned and slipped quietly down the lane. He was back almost immediately the wire cage dangling in his grip, his face tight.

'Oh Jesus!' My heart jumped. 'No Bartley, they had noth …'

He turned and grabbed me with his free hand, his eyes like points of light.

'Shut up, four eyes! Shut up and watch out for them. OK?' And he set the cage by the wall at the mouth of the lane the four 'grannies' tottering towards us, swaddled in overcoats, their chattering croon carrying easily in the dark.

They were almost on us when Bartley placed his foot on the roof of the mesh box, leaning forward to grab the flap, then I got the cold smell of petrol as he sprinkled the surging rats with it, dropping the small bottle behind him and the match caught. The night flared and rolled, squeaks and the smell of burning hair as he sprung the lid, the flaming water rats bursting forward, their squeals drowned by the screams of the 'grannies' as the six burning dancers flashed around their ankles, cutting through them, scattering them in all directions, Old Mrs Quirke's voice crying 'Devils! Devils with pink eyes!' And we slipped from the laneway, my heart like an anvil beating, my eyes full of tears as we ran.

Angelground
(Garraí na nAingeal)

Winter and wind, storm and high skies, he'd looked out at it all his life and most of the time he never thought of them, never gave them names buried there down beside the broad stone, their hidden marker. Only shadows now, hardly bodies at all, slipped to the earth in the cold darkness, his father bent to the digging, Tommy standing guard for the wrapped bundles and the neighbours' eye, the woollen blanket cut and tied with the thin cord, three times in his short years, his mother swaddled 'til their return.

He never really believed it would come to him, the encroaching town. So when Christy Convoy, in a good suit, knocked on his door and presented Tommy with a stiff rectangle of card and offered him more thousands than he could ever count off the backs of his cattle, he was truly shocked.

But during the following weeks he heard the talk on the creamery 'step' and he began to see for himself, began to read the map for the first time: Tim Kearney's land already gone, the first footings quickly set in place. Then Joe Coyne said he was selling and that was it, Christy Convoy's purse strings loosened, his broad smile and ready grip cutting through the deals, his men, with their tripods, moving across the tracts, pegging out foundations, other developers cutting their own stripes, jigsaw estates tying into each other, paper plans made flesh, the city on the move.

Sometimes on the laneway he'd look at the small hand-patch of land, 'the wood' his father had called it, the trees in leaf, or bare, or leaning from the sea-wind and he'd be back in the cold times, the dark around him like a breath, his father needing him there, the spade surgical in his grip. He could never tell Mary or the girls, kept it to himself but he knew he'd never sell it. He'd sheltered it through all Convoy's visits, his improved offers, and all the talk of never having to work again. Then he'd signed the first papers, the ten acres nearest the road, more money than he ever knew flowing into his account, their own house rebuilt and a car for himself, Mary and the girls.

And so it went, three years roughly until the day he signed away the last of it, holding on to the piece around the house and the little wood, a haven before his front door, the trees darkening it through the spring and summer, skeletons waving in the winter dark.

'What's the use of holding on to the small patch, Tommy?'

Christy Convoy sat comfortably at the kitchen table, a cup of tea and a slice of Mary's best cake before him, his blond hair swept back and his full smile offering Tommy his trust, almost. They'd remained civil through all the dealings, bargained hard, a handshake enough for Tommy, the papers and the lawyers coming afterwards, Convoy already well versed in reading the old ways.

'I sowed those trees, my own father and me, it's no use to you. What'll it hold? One house?' Tommy wasn't going to give in that easy.

'True, but why not turn it into a little park; we'd never get planning anyway. Sign it over to the Council, we'll cement the walls, they're solid enough, we have to leave the place right, keep our good name. Make it into a feature'. Convoy smiled his winning smile, nodding to Mary.

'Maybe, but it's fine as it is'.

Convoy had come back again, explaining how it was the last piece of land on the folio document, a pain having to sort it out in Dublin, signing it over now would settle it securely, forever. Protect it long after they were all gone.

Tommy had talked to Mary and the girls and after months of indecision and resistance, he'd signed the proffered document, happy with the plan, 'a feature' and Convoy's men had tidied it as he'd promised, lowered the walls and fixed a heavy barge along the top. Tommy supervised it all resting with his back to the flat stone, careful with his demands, the men hurrying to be away, new soil to break.

Now people from the filling estates could sit there and rest of an evening, young women pushing prams, their toddlers running through the few trees, their cries carrying in the summer evenings. Couples breaking their journey to the shore, reading their papers or just relaxing, their children playing in the lower branches.

And so it went, time leeching from his days as it does in its passing, the seasons becoming finite in a way that was new to him. In time he walked Mary along the laneway, through the newly road-mapped fields, the houses still strange to him, to leave her, alone before the cold altar, the girls tearful. Later he sat at their top tables as they both in turn left, binding themselves to husbands and new homes and he settled to the sitting years, wishing visits from his neighbours, the district nurse, the far too infrequent postman.

'At least you have comfort and a warm house'. Doctor Kyle had pointed out on one of his regular visits, leaving his prescription for his blood pressure and 'something to help him sleep' on the kitchen table. 'I see so much of the other story'.

Tommy had agreed. And so, with the years he still moved easily about his acre, cutting drills, growing vegetables, pruning trees, his days bothered with their rituals of regularity.

He hardly recognised young Cooley when he met him at the shops, he was driving a big jeep, Tommy glad of the lift home to his own door, Gerry talking about life in Manchester, making himself bigger than he was, the houses he'd built, office blocks even and now he was back, ten years gone but millions to be made and he'd missed his own place, so he'd start small here, a house at a time, no shortage of ready money.

'Here you are Tom'. He'd pushed the heavy door of the jeep open, holding the small bag of groceries out to Tommy as he eased himself from the high seat.

'Thanks Gerry. Thanks'. And he'd waved his walking stick in the air as the young man had manoeuvred the heavy four-wheel along the narrow laneway, slowing past the wood, the British number plate a yellow flash in the dusk.

'I see young Cooley is building a house for the Griffins'. Joe Coyne leant close to him in the back seat at nine mass one Sunday a few weeks afterwards.

'The Griffins?'

'Yes, they're building a house; the son's getting married, some young one he met in the factory'.

Tommy had smiled, wishing in a way that his own girls had been a little slower, stayed with him for a little longer. No cure for it now anyway. And on the way home he saw the black scar of the digger on the side of the low hill, the only piece the Griffins had to spare, the blocks standing in mini towers, the plastic sheets ballooning in the freshening wind.

When he reached the corner he eased himself down on to the wall, his stick resting beside him. The traffic was light, fathers off to play golf probably, some families, less than in his day, hurrying to ten mass, the children's faces pushed to the glass. He waved the odd time in return to a nod of greeting and he thought again of all those years ago, of his father leading him along the dark lane, the wheel cuts full of rainwater, the unexplained bundle, the spade in his young hands, then the digging, cutting into the tangled brown mat, the smell of earth filling his nostrils, his eyes searching the blackblur of the dark and then the hurried burial, his father's cap removed, the whispered prayer. Different times, the people afraid to raise their heads, no one ever getting above themselves. He placed his hand on the low wall, at least all was safe here and their mystery would die with him.

'So you're going to build then?' Tim Kelly said it first. Tommy was surprised. They were sitting at a table near the door of an active retirement get-together, two young lads strangling a tune, four young girls river-dancing to beat the band.

'No Tim I have no plans, too much room I have as it is. Why?'

Tim had seen the planning notice in the paper about a month before, it had to be Tommy's place, no more land left down there but his little wood.

'Then I saw young Cooley in there one morning early, measuring the frontage and I thought, maybe you were building. Last Tuesday I think, but I can't be sure though, the days are rolling now, the time is flying'.

And Tommy had mumbled that he would talk to Gerry, see what was happening and he had found the small site notice in the paper when he got home. How had he missed it?

'Yeah, I am'. Cooley stood in the shadow of Griffin's gable, the house pushing up from the rich soil, the rain pelting on the stained plastic protecting the rich brickwork. 'I bought it, fair and square'.

'Bought it?'

'Yes, from Christy Convoy, there's a man who's done fierce well. Spends most of his time in Florida now, has a house there and a swimming pool, he was only home for the races but I was lucky enough to meet him in the hospitality tent and we made the deal. I saw it that day I left you home, remember?'

'But I gave it to the city twenty years ago, signed it over myself to the Council, Convoy did it, he was all for it. He agreed to tidy it, said it was easier that way'.

'No, Convoy still owned it, my solicitors made the search, I saw the papers myself'.

'No, I, no ... Convoy promised it would go to the council and they'd maintain it. They do!'

'Look Tom, all I know is I bought it from Convoy and he was happy to sell it too. I paid enough for it but it'll be worth it in the end'. And he'd come out of the shelter of the gable to help with a batch of plasterboards, the fixers pressing on and the ceilings going in, the plasterers skimming over the new walls.

'You'd better come and see me then'. The young solicitor appeared to understand his concern over the phone. 'And bring any relevant documents', she concluded. 'Anything you have from that time'.

So he dug out everything he could find, Mary had stored everything to do with the acres he'd sold in the old wooden box safe on the high shelf, but he could find nothing to show that he'd signed the papers for the wood, no record of where the land had gone.

'No record'. Was what Miss Enright had told him also when he sat before her in the plush of her office, old Mister Waterson safely retired, his methods gone, things moving on.

'We'll do a land search', she concluded. 'It'll cost, but at least you'll know'.

And within weeks the search had come back showing he'd signed the land to Christy Convoy, as she'd feared, and no further activity after that until the recent flurry and the wood was sold.

'But he promised me there at the table! He said they'd sign it on'. He could see it in her eyes, her sympathy, but there was nothing she could do. He'd signed voluntarily, even at the insistence of his family, Mary's signature as witness. Convoy may have given his word but there was nothing written.

'Only a promise', she'd sighed. 'I see this happen all the time. These are new times, no word, handshakes are totally lost here'.

And he'd left the office, his world all behind him, his word as nothing, his only hope now that he could talk to Gerry Cooley. Almost a neighbour's son, he'd understand.

He walked the kitchen trying to clear his head, stood before his wife's picture wishing she was still there, beside it the picture of the family taken at some funfair, the girls lost to their own world, smiles as wide as heaven on their young faces. He never knew it had been so simple back then. Cooley had to understand.

'Gerry, I knew your parents, they were good people, sell it back to me, and I'll pay you all I can. I gave it to the

Council, Convoy convinced me, convinced all of us but he never passed it on. These are crooked times, Christy Convoy was thinking of himself, he promised it would be safe'.

But Cooley had moved away, shrugging. 'That was a foolish move Tom, you should have been cuter, and what do you expect?'

And that was the end to it, Tommy pleaded, then he tried offering more money but Cooley saw it as his chance, his chance to build big, a 'show' house, pillars and a fancy name, that would make his future here in his own place.

'A fancy name? After Manchester? I thought you were a big man there already?' He was sorry when he said it and Cooley could read it too.

'Who's been talking to you? I had no luck in Manchester but I'll have it here, my own people, and good labour, so don't give me that, ok?'

'But Gerry ...'

'Don't bloody well annoy me!'

Cooley's voice echoed off the drying walls, his curse buried in the hammering, the electricians chasing a late channel in the next room.

'We shook hands!' Tommy pleaded.

'Jaysus, for God's sake, those old ways don't work anymore. How can you believe that shite?'

And Tommy couldn't answer, he walked to the door shaking his head, Cooley refusing him again, shouting that the old ways were over.

'You believe that Gerry?'

'That the old ways are gone? You bet I do, there's no place for that superstitious bullshit in these times. We're moving now because all that stuff is over. I'm building, five bedrooms and a posh name, that's what people want now and if you can come up with a fancy name, you call me'.

'We'll see if that's true, we'll see'. And he had gone away head down, the possibles racing through him, the options dying fast.

The cough of the JCB brought him from the drills, the stomach-belch of diesel fumes rising through the trees. He moved slowly along the laneway, his stick unsteady, the sounds of the digging offending the silence, the yellow angle-arm moving behind the greenleaf wall. Cooley stood, legs wide apart on the top of the low wall, calling directions to the driver, lines of chalk dust sprayed on the green. He saw Tommy's unsteady progress and turned towards him, his shouts muffled but his gestures unmistakable.

'Get to fuck out of here Tommy; I don't have time for this now'. And he jumped down shouting to the driver, pointing towards the back wall.

'Yer a great man for the bad language'. Tommy was angry, his eyes on the land, he could hear his heart, the soil breaking.

'Cursing? Yeah, I am, so fuck off and let me get on with this'.

'No, that's not cursing, cursing is old, older than you or me; you'll know it when you see it. That's just bad language'.

And Gerry had told him again to 'go fuck himself' and walked away, his arm raised in dismissal.

Tommy stood for a while and watched the digging, the bucket cutting through the loam, scooping out the richness, fifty years of leaf-mould, the smell all earthy and he was back there, the night around him, his father, the hurried digging, the spade cutting through, the small bodies slipped to the earth, his mother propped and exhausted, tearful on their return.

He stood before the high shelf, he would stop this, the old ways, they were still there, scratch the surface and they would come flooding back, Europeans maybe, but down there with the dark times and the fear, the old ways were still alive. The wooden box contained all he needed, Mary's pictures and even a few of his own mother's pictures, all there with the details written on the backs, the girls growing, their relatives smiling, yeah, even a few from his mother's days.

Mary had detailed those as well, a group of his American cousins aligned before some large rented car, another one of the same group by the wall of the little wood, their names written in his own mother's slow hand, fading now, all the names listed and below the list she'd written 'taken at Garraí na nAingeal'. Tommy could remember it then, his mother whispering the name, his father's head inclined towards her, his eyes fixed on her, and yes, he sensed it now, the name growing personal again, taking on more meaning for him. Now he was ready.

There was no moon, the digger stood angled, ill at ease almost, a gaunt yellow ribcage, ghostly in the darkness; he stumbled on the uneven soil, the stickiness heavy on his boots, the box awkward in his grip. The newly dug trenches fenced the small site, all the four footings cut to their required depth, a mountain of soil pushed to one end. He found the flat stone in the low wall, his bones aching and the bottle of water heavy in his coat, his joints stiff from the cold.

He eased down, sitting on the edge of the trench, the bottle cap proving tricky in the darkness, the capsules sticky on his dry tongue, the water dripping on his waistcoat as he drank, the contents of the container slipping easy. The nick of the angled blade slicing into his bare flesh hardly hurt at all, wrist vein and vertical cut, his blood a dark overcoat in the shallow trench, soaking, a red wave easing him down. He would sleep now, he had family around him, he could sense them, in his mind they shuffled to be near.

All his history was here with him, he rested his head on the old box, placed the faded picture on his chest. He felt his blood wrap itself around him, its stickiness warmed him. He had a name for Gerry's house, a firm line drawn through his mother's hand, 'Angelground' written in his own.

BEING MISTER SMITH

'Hello Ciara!' Robbie was out from behind his desk almost tripping himself on the tangle of computer cables, his arms outstretched. 'Great way to finish Friday', and he pecked her lightly on the cheek.

'Do I get a proper welcome back kiss?' She smiled right at him before turning to take in the work-stations stretching away from his desk towards the drinking fountain at the back.

'Look who's here!' He turned to Marie the office manager and watched as they hugged and shook hands in the doorway. Ciara had that lovely way of almost curtseying as she laughed that made her look all the more beautiful.

'Well Robbie, how's things here? Tell me all the news'. And they settled down to a twenty minute rant of lost business, office spats and who would succeed old Mister Wilson if he ever decided to retire, which was by no means a certainty as they agreed, Robbie joking about wooden stakes, garlic and midnight, before she moved off to visit her colleagues at their workstations.

He watched her moving from station to station, fellow workers rising to greet her, some exchanging hugs. At one desk she leant across to take the mouse, clicking on a section of the screen, leaning even closer to find the required remedy, her long hair swinging towards the blue light before straightening and smiling at the proffered thanks.

After that he drifted back to his desk and fussed with the mass of papers there. The back of the week was truly broken now, Friday afternoons were always a slack time, he knew it and the other staff knew it, their shoulders easing towards the weekend.

At five thirty she was back at his office door and they talked about her move to the Dublin office, her promotion and the new regime. 'I love it', she smiled. 'And I have you to thank'.

He dismissed her thanks with a wave. 'Cream to the top I have to say', he laughed as the time clock chimed and the lights began to flicker and gap-tooth in the long ceiling.

'Time for a coffee?' Marie appeared at the door and Ciara checked her watch.

'Ok. I'll just finish with Robbie here and I'll follow you to Rio's', she called, as Marie pushed through the doors.

'Thanks again Robbie, I really mean it', she smiled and he nodded.

'How long are you staying?'

'Just for the weekend, I need a good night out'. She ran her fingers through her long hair absentmindedly as she spoke. He sensed the unasked question just hanging there, waiting. Or was he just imagining?

'See the girls; I'll be in Duffs later for a few if they really start to get you down'.

'I might do that', she smiled, holding his gaze for a long moment and then she was gone.

Robbie spent a little time tidying his desk; he filed the disks and eased his personal computer into e-mode for the weekend. 'Uisce faoi thalamh', he smiled at one of the few Irish language phrases he could still remember from his schooldays. He knew it could be literally translated as 'water underground', but related more to intrigue, political or social, than to anything else yet it always reminded him now of all those computers silently moving masses of information out there somewhere beyond the occupied spaces, the places he understood.

Driving home, nose to tail, he thought back to the time when Ciara had gone for the promotion at the head office of the firm. He had to push her at the beginning, telling her she would be great, how the job was made for her, she had the qualifications, all the letters after her name, how she could do it with her eyes closed. He had even driven her to Dublin the day of the interview, he was going anyway to meet a client, but it gave her confidence.

After the interview was over he met her in the canteen. He expected her to be down and a little apprehensive but instead she'd gripped his arm telling him about the job and how she had to get it. Her competitiveness had surprised him, her fists clinched; the combative nature of her approach.

'I know I can do it now, I know it!'

He smiled. Yes, he had no doubts on that count, he could see it in the clearness of her eyes and they both knew it.

When the news arrived she'd hugged him in full view of everyone, her slender legs swinging free of the carpet.

'Well done! You show them'. Knowing that she would, knowing that in some way she was harder than he or anyone else would have guessed and he'd felt good that now she would get the chance.

Kathy was at home stirring something in a saucepan when he came through the door.

'Hard day?' Her perfunctory kiss stirred nothing.

'Yeah, yeah the usual. You out later?'

'Yeah, staff-night, the girls are going to 'The Coconut'; it's Sheilagh's hen-night. We'll probably go on to a club. You?'

'Duffs, the usual, I'll probably see Mike'. He knew Mike was off on a cross-country weekend chasing through some forest or other with a stopwatch and a compass swinging from his neck, spindle legged in his bad shorts. Orienteering; he could never understand the need himself, except maybe it could be that forty-something wish to keep the bad world at bay. 'Be immortal' it said, 'drive back time, for a little longer, even if…'

Duffs was jumping with that strange mix of businessmen, students and general misfits that rarely rubbed shoulders anywhere else but there. Behind the bar Big Richie was doing his usual thing; filling four pints at once, spinning mixers and touching the optics with his firm kiss. Terri, looking great in a tight top and jeans was moving at her normal leisurely pace, pulling pints and giving lip to the punters.

He took his regular stand behind the 'blind' counter, a relic of the time when Duffs had been a grocery shop as well as a bar. Big Richie passed the cold beer across with a sly wink and jiggled the coins in his cupped hands to the rhythm of the band blaring from the speakers.

'Wild out there tonight son!'

'Yeah, looks wild in here too'.

'Full moon?' Big Richie joked, dropping the coins in the till. The crowd was surging with a mind of its own, faces came and went and he nodded at some, ignoring others, the pints slipping slowly down his throat towards easiness.

'Hiya!' She stood before him in a short dress that was way too tight even for her figure and a pair of black strapless sandals that gave the impression of having been painted on her tiny feet.

'Ciara!' He caught Big Richie's eye.

'Vodka', she smiled and the big man did his little dance before the optics, glass flashing, hands blurring, the slick spirit bubbling through.

'I left the girls in Talons', she shouted in his ear, her breath smelling of nothing, her small hand squeezed in a fist as she stood on tiptoe. He'd had four pints; he did the back count, but was he drunk? He didn't think so, but he didn't want to confuse the vital signs.

After that they talked above the din, the music sliding from blues to jazz and back again, the rounds coming easy. Once he thought he recognised a familiar eye in the crowd but even though he leant closer to Ciara the eye, the bald spot and the halo of grey hair had disappeared.

Towards closing time there was a disturbance near the front door but the crowd closed around it and he used the moment to slip out to the toilets.

'Back in a minute', he breathed as he eased past Ciara, their bodies brushing from thigh to shoulder.

'I'll be here', she smiled and just for a blinktime he thought of Kathy.

The rusty pipe snaked from the ceiling to the urinals and he rested his head against it for the coldness it would bring.

'Are you being Mister Smith?' His piss jumped off the tiles at the deep voice.

'Ah, hiya Bartley'. He turned to the ravaged face, the grey curls framing the bald dome. Yes, he had seen the eye.

'Long time no see'.

He considered shaking hands but changed his mind.

'Are you?'

'Wha?'

'C'mon. Are you being Mister Smith? That's not your Kathy'.

'No'. He shrugged. 'She's from work, just met her by accident'.

'She's a looker, great rack. Spotted her an hour ago myself. You'll introduce us then?'

'Ciara. This is Bartley Elwood, we were at school together'.

'Same class but Robbie was a little behind me in some ways love. We lived on the same road when we were kids'. And he took her hand and seemed reluctant to let go. 'I often kicked his arse'. he nodded. 'He was very good at running but I caught him the odd time'.

Robbie avoided his eye. There was another surge near the door, the crowd splitting before it.

'Here they go again!' Bartley nodded.

'Who?'

'Ah, couple of young lads, the blond lad and the skinhead, shaping up all night. See the girl sitting in the corner with the big assets? She has them pumped, been playing them off all night'. He kept a weather eye on the situation, his gaze straying to Ciara, his thick shoulders flexing under the expensive coat.

'Here we go!' He turned towards them. 'They're going to the multi-storey to settle it'.

'How do you know?'

'My men do the doors here. If there's trouble they suggest going to the car park, it keeps it away from Duffs and it keeps it away from us too'.

Ciara was straining to see, standing on her tiptoes she leant close to Robbie, her small hand steadying on his shoulder. Bartley noticed and caught his eye.

'C'mon, there's nothing like a good floorshow to finish off the night. The entrance stairs are next-door', and he was off through the crowd. Ciara took Robbie's arm and began to follow. He held on, the beer making his feet big and unsteady, the floor feeling all uneven and out of tune.

'We could ...?' He took her slim waist. 'The car is down by the docks'. She turned to him, smiling, her eyes shining in the bar light.

'Emm, later, let's see the floorshow first'. She was backing away, a smile playing on her lips, her long hair shining, the heavy drums beating in their heads.

The crowd took the stairs towards Level 2, the cold steps echoing to their urgings of support. Robbie could see Bartley just ahead, one of his men at his shoulder, shaven-headed, clearing his path through the rush.

By the time Ciara and Robbie pushed through the double doors to Level 2 the fight had already started, the crowd forming a tight ring under the cold roof lights.

'Ciara?' He tried to hold on to her thin waist. 'C'mon'. He tried to brush her hair away from where the ends were sticking in the corner of her mouth but she pulled him towards the circle, Bartley pushing ahead, his goon steadying the surge of the human ring with his tattooed arms.

Robbie braced himself as the crowd swung towards him and he saw the fighters for the first time. Blondie's shirt was already gone as he struggled to swing a roundhouse punch at the bloody face before him. But Skinhead was too fast, ducking below the swing, his kick connecting with

Blondie's ribs before they clinched and crashed to the concrete floor.

The crowd closed in forming a heaving crater above the struggling pair. They were still locked together trying to knee each other; their legs locked in a straining tangle. Blondie saw his chance, his hair swinging as he butted Skinhead between the eyes, the crack of bone on bone momentarily silencing the crowd. He'd opened a deep gash across the bridge of Skinhead's nose, blood spattering his face as they struggled to their feet, still locked together.

Ciara was gripping his arm now in a fierce grip, her nails sinking into the leather of his sleeve. He could see Bartley Elwood forcing the crowd back, his helper doing the same.

'Give them room! Give them room!' Bartley roared as they swung in a bloody lock towards the railings. Skinhead swung again, landing a punch on Blondie's jaw, sending him skidding along the oily surface, the crowd baying as he fell. Skinhead pawed at his eyes as he tried to clear his vision and swung another vicious kick into Blondie's exposed ribs. The crowd groaned as Blondie vomited, his face in the oily mess, curling into a ball to avoid another kick.

Robbie tried to pull Ciara back but she was in the front row now, her short dress taut across her buttocks as she urged Skinhead on, her small fists raised. Skinhead seemed to hear her, his boot high above Blondie's exposed head but Blondie rolled just in time as he stamped down hard, slipping on the mixture of beer vomit and oil. Blondie regained his balance; his knee connecting with Skinhead's exposed jaw, the crunch of bone, a crack in the empty car park.

Skinhead hit the ground out cold and the crowd groaned; they knew the fight was over, but Blondie wasn't finished, he lurched again and stood swaying above his opponent. The kick came so quickly that no one could stop him. It connected just below the ear, a tooth shot from Skinhead's sagging jaw and lodged in the pool at Ciara's feet.

Bartley was in; pinning Blondie's spattered arms to his sides and hauling him away, the crowd parting in the slow silence.

'Check him!' Bartley shouted to his bouncer and, for just a second, Robbie heard the bubble of fear in his voice, saw it in his eyes. The man knelt beside the unconscious Skinhead feeling for a pulse in his throat.

'He's out but still pumping, jaw's broken, I'll phone for the ambulance'.

Bartley nodded. The girl who had caused the whole affray threw herself on the ground beside the still unconscious Skinhead calling 'Gerry, Gerry', between sobs, trying to stem the flow of blood with a tattered tissue, her friends kneeling to comfort her.

Robbie eased his shoulders against a pillar; he felt sick, the smell of beer vomit in his nostrils, the hot bile rising in his throat. Ciara pressed her slim knee between his shaking legs. She smelt so good, her knee sliding upwards, her lips brushing against his flushed cheek.

'Robbie, are you all right? We should go now'' He held her fiercely, squeezing her to him, feeling her pelvis thrust against him, her knee coming up slowly into his crotch.

'No!'

She looked at him confused, her eyes focussing as if for the first time.

'No', he whispered. 'Wait', pushing her away, his hands held out before him.

'Robbie?' She tried to touch his arm.

'Just leave it Ciara, leave it for now, ok?'

'Robbie?' Her plea only made it worse. She shivered, rubbing her bare arms. He took a step away, turning as Bartley Elwood approached and placed his expensive coat across her shoulders.

'Time to run again Robbie, time to run'. He smiled, his eyes still glinting from the fight.

'Ciara?' Robbie was confused.

She didn't answer, didn't meet his eye. She stood head down, the expensive coat around her shoulders, swaying slightly, moving the tooth, its halo of red flesh still attached, with the polished toe of her dainty black strapless sandal.

Sparrowpicker

McGann came by in the Transit out of the blue and Bernie glared, just daring Jacky to refuse. Two or three days work building walls, labouring in a quiet suburban back garden, away from prying eyes, well away from losing his benefits.

'A hundred a day and bring your own food'. McGann had conceded. He was a solid block of a man, not unlike the building he did, solid and without compromise, never a man to waste words and Jacky had hunched in the back of the van with Hagan and a young foreign lad, who looked Polish, thin face of hunger, big eyes of need. The smell of diesel was heavy from the rag-strewn floor, the mixer hunchbacked with the shovels, rattling along behind in the muck-thick trailer.

Thirty minutes out, the radio set to some local station, all goodwill and backslapping, the van swung easy through the gates, McGann tooling it around by the side of the low-slung bungalow, Jacky and Hagan stepped from the sliding side door, the Polish kid unhooking the trailer, winding the jack-wheel to lift the load clear of the tow-bar, all business fit and ready to work.

The bungalow was in good order, neat and well painted. It sat in a semi-circle of mature trees, roses climbing the curtain wall, neighbouring houses only a rumour. There were even doves patrolling the ridge tiles. It smelled of money, the base picked out in terracotta which carried through to the large garden-room, all glass and light, the flower borders, in early summer, heavy with growth.

McGann pointed out the foundations already in place, trenched and set, one hill of soil piled neatly on a couple of old doors, the blocks stacked in neat towers on the short grass and they swung into action, Hagan set the lines, scraped the trowels while Jacky and the Pole got the mixer going, horsing it into position and filling it from the trailer before they shovelled the rest of the sand from the trailer onto the heavy plastic. McGann sliced through the first of the cement bags, tipped half of the contents into the drum followed by the end of the tangled hose spouting water and they settled in to the regular rhythm of the day.

Around midday when Hagan was four courses up the patio door opened and a blonde woman, probably in her late forties crossed the lawn with a stacked plate of scones and a mixture of mugs which she set down on top of one of the rectangles of blocks. Then she returned to the house for a large pot of tea and a carton of milk. Jacky liked the way she moved, honed and easy, thought 'gym' or maybe 'swim', but still, he wouldn't mind, no way ...

McGann thanked her and Jacky thought he caught the name but he couldn't be sure. The Pole ate with a grim consistency, his face to the flowers, Jacky watching him as the blonde woman refilled their cups and chatted to McGann.

'Seldom we get treated like this'. McGann remarked, thanking her before she returned to the house, McGann assuring her that they would definitely be finished by Wednesday, but only if he kept 'these lads' from slackening off.

'I'm off for more sand for the plastering', he looked at Jacky. 'Keep the mixer going'. He swilled the last of the tea and scattered the tea-leaves across the grass, while Jacky tipped another half bag of cement into the mixer and added the water.

It grew hotter as the sun rose above them, the garden sheltered, the sky clear. The dust streaked his arms as he loaded the mix before tipping it, the Pole carrying the cement to Hagan, then feeding him blocks; sweat beading on his brown back, the walls rising along the yellow line.

Jacky removed his shirt. The cooking smell of the flat mixed with his own body smell, last night's Guinness and cigarettes percolated in the sunny heat as he shovelled, the sand hitting the spinning drum, the Pole ferrying the buckets of mix to Hagan, the wall rising, pillars forming, the heavy thud of the lump hammer, cement breaking as Hagen cut halves, the zing of the bolster chisel biting into the pitted hardness of the block.

'Hey!' Jacky eyed the Pole.

'Hey, whatever your name is, slow down to fuck. We'll get three days here anyway, don't kill yerself'. But the Pole only told him his name was Piotr and he was gone again, two buckets poured from the mixer's eye, keeping them upright and steady as he walked, stiff-armed, the tendons like steel wires in his thin arms, before tipping the cement onto the board, Hagan sinking the trowel in.

'Fucker, cunt ...'

'Ahhm ...'

Jacky hadn't seen the man standing behind him. He was tall with a salt and pepper crew-cut, a good suit, a white shirt and tie and now Jacky had been caught out. This was Mister Blonde. The man gave no hint that he'd heard him.

'Hard at it?' The question breaking the held silence.

'Yeah, coming along nicely now, we got a good day for it'.

'I'm Kevin Hewitt, is Mister McGann around?'

'Gone for sand. You want the shed re-plastered he was saying?'

'Yes. It looks bad, bad job the first day ever. I'd like to plaster it up and paint it maybe. Sow climbers there, something like that'. The name had to be more than a coincidence. It had to be.

'Have you lived here long Mister Hewett?' Jacky eyed him, trying not to show too keen an interest. This was only chat.

'We bought here in 'eighty-nine, thought I was paying a fortune at the time, look at things now'.

'Yeah must be worth a lot all right'. He thought of his own flat near the Docks, two rooms, rented cheap, no one else would bother, the landlord happy to let them rot, the constant smell of food, Bernie mostly trying her best but she was a lazy bitch, too many chips and burgers, even the younger kids were looking fat, piles of clothes everywhere. He supposed it was better since Shay had moved out, gone, a sulk on him since he'd been a teenager. They'd never gotten on, maybe they'd had him too young, and it hadn't been planned, anything but ... maybe ... maybe bollocks.

Jacky told Hewitt how he lived in town himself, down near the docks and used the opportunity to ask if he was local, finding out that he was from Sligo.

'Sligo, just outside the town, I moved here after college, I enjoyed the university here and I got a job with O'Reilly's, the engineers'. Hewitt studied the wall of the shed again, rubbing the dusty finish with his hand.

'Oh yeah, I've heard of them'. He'd been right, same name, same part of the country as that little fucker, had to be some relation. Then McGann had swung the van around by the side of the bungalow and Kevin Hewitt had moved off, heel-tipping the grit from the soles of his expensive shoes.

'Bastard …' Had to be the same family at least, probably a son. Hewitt. He could still see the blur of movement, the sudden shoulder dip, and the blow between his eyes before he could even swing, the other bouncers moving in as he lay struggling on the wet road like a crab upturned on a rock, the long queue of patrons turning towards the fracas, the raucous voices of the men, and the giggles of all the leggy women.

And he hadn't been drunk, sure, he'd had a few, but Eamonn had been worse and Toolers too and they'd both gotten in. Hewitt, that was the name the head-bouncer had called him, little fucker, good shoulders though and fast, the punch spreading his nose, the sticky ripeness of the blood mixing with the puke as he wretched.

They'd rough-gripped him over to the railings then while he was still struggling until the head-bouncer told him to go or 'Sligo' would phone the police. What were the chances? Had to be good, he'd find out if it killed him, the shovel ripping swiftly into the fresh cement bag.

'Here!' McGann was coming across the lawn towards him.

'Keep it tidy, keep it tidy. I told you. Look, get started on the shed, I'll do this'. And he handed him the small pick. 'Rough it up for the plastering, we'll get to it tomorrow'.

He was still sparrowpicking the rough plaster of the shed after the lunch-break when Mrs Hewitt came across the lawn with a basket and began shaking the creases out of a stack of white shirts before pinning them to the rotary clothesline. Her arms were tanned, the fingers long and delicate, the pegs slipping easy, pinning the wet clothes.

'Hot now'. Jacky eyed her as she worked.

'Yes', she mused, pausing to look at the sky. 'A lovely day. They say it's the hottest this year so far. Would you like a drink, orange maybe?'

He smiled, that would be nice and she returned carrying a large jug and glasses for Hagan and the Pole and then she poured a glass for Jacky.

'What exactly are you doing there?' She pointed at the wall.

'Sparrowpicking. Ah, picking holes in the old plaster, roughing it up, with this, it's a roofing hammer, for slating, the point digs into the plaster, makes little holes, then we coat it in plasticiser, mix it with the plaster and it sticks. Good as new, better actually'.

She started to move away, he'd ask now. 'I knew someone called Hewitt once, I still do actually; he works where I bring my wife dancing'.

'Is it the club downtown, Curly Tate's?'

'Yeah, we're the oldest there but she likes it'.

'Yes, Curly Tate's. He's Kevin's nephew, Jason. He's in college here and he earns a little extra on the door. Kevin is not happy about it, thinks it's too dangerous. What do you think?' she moved closer to him, looking concerned. He could see the fine lines near her eyes, the crinkle of them.

'Dangerous? No I never saw any trouble there, all twenty-something's, oh and two in their forties', he smiled.

'Does she like it?'

'Who?'

'Your wife, you said …'

'Oh yeah, Bernie loves it, keeps her in great shape, wears me out dancing, she does'. And he smiled as Mrs Hewitt moved away. He smiled twice, once at the idea of

Bernie dancing in the first place and again at the notion of bringing her to Curly Tate's. Fuck that, she'd beat herself to death, the sag on her. That'd be one for the lads to take the piss at. No, and he smiled again remembering how he'd often mingled with the young ones at the long bar trying his luck. Never even bothered to remove his wedding ring anymore, lots of takers now for the no-strings-attached one-nighters.

'Pick it closer'. McGann took the roofing hammer roughly from his grip to demonstrate, moving over a small patch of wall, the point digging into the old plaster, small eyes gouged out, and the bird-beaks of plaster sticking in the hairs of his arm. 'Here and keep your mind on the job'.

It was always the same, always the fucking same. No matter where he worked, some bollocks always showing him up, always. Jacky didn't need this, he'd tell him to shove his fucking job but McGann was handy with his fists, had planted a lot of good men.

But now he knew who Hewitt was, a fucking student, and a little bastard. There'd be again, he promised. And he could hear the voice from that night, saying how he didn't think 'sir was in a fit state'. Telling him that maybe if he had something to eat he'd be ok and pointing out the coffee shop across the street.

Jacky had laughed right at him, asking him if he thought Jacky was some country gobshite in from the bogs to be sent across the street for sandwiches and a large mug of tea. Except that he'd be the mug because by the time he got back the doors of the club would be long closed. And he'd pushed his face closer to Hewitt's.

'Am I pissed, am I?'

Hewitt had asked him not to raise his voice and Jacky had made to swing except he never saw it coming, not really, until all the sounds exploded with the blow, his mind focussing on the whistle-sound in his ears and the sick feeling as he had hit the hard road. Fucker, fucker, fucker, he'd settle him; he would, if he had to wait a year. The bastard.

'A for God's sake! What are you at?' McGann grabbed the pick from his hand. 'Look at the state of the wall, willya. What are you thinking of?'

Jacky's eyes focussed on the pitted wall, plaster wafers littering the ground, the raw block visible.

'Jesus Jacky, do you want the few days or not? Bernie said that Communion was coming up; I thought you needed the money?'

'Bernie?'

'Fuck it Jacky, do you have a child for Communion or not?'

'Yeah, Alannyah, what's that got to do ...'

'Bernie met my wife in Aldi or Lidl the other day and said you could do with the work, a little extra to help pay?'

Jacky rubbed his chin. Bernie the bitch, fucken' charity work, if ...

'Here, get back on the mixer, you're here now and that's it, I'll finish this'.

Bitch, he'd give her Communion. He'd give her charity.

Piotr was tipping the last of the mix from the drum and he eyed him as he passed, his stare moving on when Jacky paused. They were everywhere now, these bloody Poles, thin as lathes, the fit fuckers and showing the Paddies up. No slacking anywhere because there were half a dozen of them waiting, just waiting to move in. And all that builders' talk about how you'd find them outside the gates before eight o'clock, even before the siren went. Maybe it was true but fuck that, he'd not be pushed around in his own country. He would not.

He tipped the last of the cement into the open drum and shovelled in the sticky sand, the drum spinning the mix as he added the water from the hose. He continued to add the sand a shovel at a time as the mix firmed. This would be it for today probably. They were out of cement anyway, as he began to scrape the sand into a tidy pile, the sun prickling the sheltered skin of his back.

That was another thing, these foreign women, brown all over even after working here for a year, never understood that. They'd talked about it in the bar, standing back from the wooden counter, and three pints before them, Eamonn, Toolers and himself, no Paddy redneck on them like the Irish girls. Good times.

Mrs Hewitt was at the patio door again. He was feeling full, could do with taking a dump.

'Could I use your toilet ma'am?' He made a big show of wiping his shoes, getting the last of the sand off, Mrs Hewitt telling him it was fine and not to worry. She smiled as he squeezed past.

'Jason is doing engineering at the University'.

'Who?'

'Jason, you thought you might know him? Here he is when he won some shoot-fighting competition last year'. She pointed to a picture on the sideboard. 'They say he's quite good'.

Jacky wiped the sweat and grit from his forehead and temples.

'Yes, that's him alright, Shoot-fighting?'

'Yes. He's been training for years, it's a dangerous sport, and he messes with the kids whenever he comes to visit. I suppose it's no harm to be able to defend yourself? He spent last summer training in Holland'.

'Holland?'

'Yes, training, he got a scholarship from the University, in sport. He fights for them. In competitions?'

'Oh? Where's the toilet?' He needed time.

'Yes, yes, use the bathroom; it's down the hall on the right'.

The bathroom was cool after the heat of the garden. It smelt of lavender and fresh soap, a blue glass dish and a pottery bowl full of petals on the sill. He relieved himself quickly, the burger and Guinness of the night before, wiping himself and belting up the grimy work jeans again. He turned to the sink passing the soap between his wet hands. He smelt of ripe sweat and wet cement, the skin on his shoulders reddening from the sun. He bent towards the mirror trying to see his shoulders, turning towards the light, he'd be burnt tomorrow but he didn't care. Fucken' shoot fighting.

He looked around for a towel and found it folded neatly on the towel-rail, it smelled of newness but then, he knew it would. He dried his hands quickly, thinking again of Bernie and McGann and that little fucker leaving him on his back like an upturned crab, scrabbling on the wet street. Fucken' engineer.

Quickly he unbuckled his jeans again. They dropped to his ankles with his jocks. He could hear the choke-beat of his own heart, saw his eyes dark-rimmed, reflected in the circular mirror, pressing the fresh towel to his face. Bending bowlegged he passed the soft towel roughly between his sweaty legs, bringing it close to his face again, inhaling himself, rubbing it hard once more into his crotch, hard between his legs, wiping his arse and balls with it, before folding it neatly and placing it back on the silvered towel-rail. Quickly he dressed himself and flushed the toilet. Fuck them.

There was little said going home in the van. Piotr sat facing the doors, his eyes on the traffic through the dirty rear window. As ever Hagan said nothing and appeared to be sleeping and Jacky sat hunched, his stare focussed on the mixture of rags and papers on the floor of the van.

He climbed out and came to the driver's window when McGann pulled in at the end of his road.

'You can pay me now, I won't be there tomorrow'.

McGann eased his bulk from the tattered seat, zipping the sleeveless fleece, pulling a fold-over wallet from his trouser pocket, his eyes on Jacky's shut face.

'You sure?'

'Yeah, you have Petey the Pole'.

'Piotr is Latvian.

'Like I fucking care, he's not Irish, is he?'

'A hundred then'. McGann picked five twenties from the leather wallet and passed them over. Jacky muttered his thanks and went to move but McGann placed his ham-like arm against the side of the van blocking him.

'Jacky, don't take this any further. Ok?'

'What?'

'What I said about the Communion. I thought you knew. I thought you were keen for the work. Ok?'

'Fuck you', Jacky spat. 'Fuck you!'

McGann swung his closed fist, crashing it against the sheet-metal side of the Transit. He held the tattered wallet an inch from Jacky's face.

'No! I don't want to hear anymore talk about it again, not from you, or from my wife either, never. From no one, now, do you understand?'

Jacky looked at the heavy fist, grey streaks of dried cement between the reddened knuckles. He kept his eyes on the van as McGann eased back into the driver's seat meeting Piotr's eyes in the rear-view mirror, he nodded once and eased the Transit into gear.

Wall

I was three weeks sleeping on Joe Clancy's floor with no sign of any improvement, eating from tins and drinking from tins as well, with no chance of getting back inside my own front door until I cleaned up my act, or apologised, or begged, or something, but I didn't know what and Morley was on my case at work, calling for more all the time, raising the job-count, giving me hell.

Joe Clancy was fine about it. He was single anyway and he was between women as well. He'd head off out at night, happy to be in a bar and sometimes I'd tag along and he'd lose me after the first bar or maybe the second, easing his body between two young things, his eyes on their breasts, his fingers in the curve of their backs and I'd sit there drinking. Tipping fifty wasn't the best time to be breaking up and bingeing and losing my family and my home and, I suppose, my wife too.

'How's your count Robbie?' Joe would ask, knowing that he was fine, covering well over the required number of cases a day and even though I was the senior man I was the one under pressure and struggling with the job. The biggest drawback was that I couldn't sign off on the work done. I'd missed the qualification when I should have got it, senior man, but at the beck and call. I was billing all I could and Morley was coining it for the bosses after leapfrogging over all of us, everyone hungry for new accounts, business booming all the time, the paperwork piling up.

'Not so great'. This was the best I could muster, knowing I was getting the heavy clients, knowing Morley was fixing it, clients with baggage and clients with history and money lost here and there. Some of them had memory loss too, which was only cured when the Revenue got on their backs and some steel-rimmed woman seated herself like a north wind in their office and brought out paper they thought had gone down with the Titanic and dropped it on their desks.

'It slipped my mind', became the mantra and then I'd have to declare that my client could 'now recall with some clarity' and would only be too happy to make a settlement and Morley would purse his purple, liverish lips and look at me, 'not good enough Mr King' written large across his flabby jowls.

'Maybe I'll hand that over to Miss Crowe', was his usual threat and I'd look through his slanting blinds at Carrie Crowe or 'The Crow' as she was referred to by Joe, all new and qualified and full of vim, perched at her corner desk. I'd say there was no need and scurry back to my cubbyhole and begin again.

And then the annual office party came around and I had to phone Kathy to beg for my good suit and she said I could come around and collect it but only when Dessie was out at football because if we had another row he'd get upset again and he was doing badly enough at school as it was and fighting on the bus and I was a selfish bastard and she knew it and I knew it too.

I stood in front of the wardrobe mirror and smoothed my tie, I could hear Kathy downstairs on the phone, she'd been on it when I arrived and I knew it was her sister and this was her protection if I misbehaved. I straightened the tie and checked the cufflinks and had another sip from the naggin of Powers and slipped it back into my breast pocket, over my heart and out of sight.

The party would be a ball-breaker, with Morley mad to show how he was blending the boss and big brother roles. He'd gazumped all of us, myself included, when old Wilson retired and here he was, weaving a safety-net around us, bringing us with him, even if we could all see right through him. He was fucking with our heads too, slipping new practices into place and new ways of doing things. Now he was running these early-morning meetings, Carrie Crowe all preened beside him, where your arse could get savaged even before you got to sit down, sip a cup of coffee and read the agenda.

So I slipped the naggin back into my pocket and stood at the front bedroom window, resting my palms on the painted sill and tried to work out the lay of the land, not as it looked now but maybe eighty or a hundred years before, my eye following the new road, how it cut through the meander of the older one. You could see the new housing estates springing up off it, but the old map of it was still there, the curves of briars and stone walls, even a cluster of old ruins outlining it on its way towards the shore.

The 'Seasand Road' the locals called it and I tried to follow where it stitched in and out, passing under the railway tracks and the big house in the woods off in the distance, and around by the older houses, and I could hear Kathy giving it ninety, still on the phone, waiting to get me out of the house, waiting to get me out of her life.

I'd been having a few and a few more over the previous nine months or so, I suppose; dealing with the shift I call it. It's like there's a day comes when you just feel that the deck has moved, everything has gone up a gear and you can feel the push, the extra expected of you. No one says it to you or knocks an anvil on your head or anything but you feel it pulling you back and there's an extra spring to everyone, and a tightness to the whole team.

You find yourself taking down books from the shelf you haven't touched in years and checking procedures and asking Joe Clancy for the most up-to-date tax-law print-offs and reading them, just in case. Or you find Carrie Crowe just looking at you like something that you'd find growing on old bread when you look up from your screen and your desk is all cluttered with paper and half-eaten sandwiches and everything astray.

I took the shortcut towards the bus stop, around by 'old Tommy's' house, it was boarded up now since he died, the weeds silent in their movement but reclaiming it all the same. Someone had cracked their first window and the decay would accelerate now, his daughters settled away, calling the odd weekend to check the locks.

He was the only one who welcomed us when we moved in, calling to the door, a fresh-faced man in his early seventies, to tell us if we needed anything where to come. That must be over ten years ago now and almost three years since they found him frozen in the footings of the new house where Cooley the builder lives now, a painted name and the empty pill bottles on his chest, no blood left in his veins, a waxen smile on his blue lips.

'Cooley'll never sell it, not after that'. I'd heard the comment one morning standing for the early bus, two old women, scarfed and sacred in their beliefs. And they'd been right. Cooley moved in with his wife and children as client after client had heard how it was haunted. And even though they laughed and shrugged when they met with Cooley, the wife or partner or girlfriend would squeeze the husband's arm and say 'we'll think about it and get back to you', all of them agreeing that the last thing they needed was a body in the foundations even if everyone knew old Tommy was safely buried in the cemetery along with his wife.

While I was waiting for the bus Dessie and two of his friends turned the corner, on me before he saw me. He said something to the lads, shuffled over and I asked him how he was.

'Fine'. And he kicked the bus stop with his trainer, his football boots and dirty shirt in a plastic bag.

'How's the soccer going?' I was trying here.

'Did you see mum?' His gaze was hard and I knew she'd been at it and I fumbled for an answer.

'Did you give her the money?'

I had given her most of what was owed and said yes.

'All of it?' He was getting big now, filling out and still only fourteen.

'Almost. But that's between mum and me'. The other two laughed at something and he glanced in their direction. I didn't care much for the look of them, razored heads, cold eyes, but what could I say?

'Almost? Dad you don't have a car now, only mum has a licence and you're living in town too and Mum has all the bills'.

'That's between mum and me'. I knew I'd lost my licence. He moved closer.

'Dad …'. Then I saw him catch his breath and mine too. 'You're still drinking, I can smell it'.

And I tried to take his arm, I wanted to slip him twenty but he pulled away and the bus swung in at the bus stop and he joined his friends, all of them watching me as I fumbled for the change.

So I was having a few, snuggled in the back of a pub on Shop Street and knowing I had a dinner to go to and sit through and listen to the New Testament according to Morley. They'd be meeting up in Hartigans for the backslapping, but I'd skip that. I'd nodded a Guinness to the barman in case he was chatty and now I was elbows up and happy, halfway down the second pint, the creamed glass smoothing everything. Even Kathy's face was easing away from me, how she'd looked when I slipped downstairs and left the envelope on the table. She could spot the flat of the naggin of Powers in my breast pocket warming my heart and she'd turned her back and said, 'he's just leaving now and he's drunk', into the phone.

They were all well seated when I arrived, the room packed to the rafters, with Christmas lights and rampant good cheer. I spotted our bunch in the far corner, the waiters fussing with the laminated menus and despite myself I had to sit one seat down from Morley. He put his hand on my shoulder, calling down the table to one of the lads, something about the wine and he just left his hand there like I could wait, then he moved off without saying anything, calling to a waiter laden down with a tray of wine bottles.

At least there was an empty chair between him and me, I'd chosen the lesser of the evils, easing in beside Tommy Mooney, who only ever talked about work but he seemed to have visited Hartigans and was smiling into space at something funny and twirling his empty wine glass airily.

Morley came towards us slapping fistfuls of bottles on the tables, four to a group, telling us to drink up and there was more where that came from.

'He'll not have to tell me twice'. Tommy Mooney leant in, filled my glass to the brim. Maybe things would be fine after all.

'You'd swear he was paying for it himself, the bollocks'. Joe Clancy whispered on his way to the toilets.

'Ah, whatever, we'll help him spend it'. I drained my glass, Tommy Mooney already ahead, smiling his big-toothed grin at me, the red stain of it, as we watched Morley working the tables, slapping backs, getting close to the women, patting ass.

'He's some fucken eejit'. Mooney was on a mission and well down his third glass when Carrie Crowe slipped into the vacant chair between Morley's and mine.

'Mister King, are you well?'

'Ah Miss Crowe, were you delayed?'

'No, I was at the ladies'. And she slipped the napkin like a shroud across her thin knees. This was going to be even worse than I'd expected so I clinked glasses with Tommy Mooney, may as well be pissed as miserable and he winked back or maybe his eyelid had started to droop, it was difficult to tell.

Morley was back as the starters arrived, we'd all more or less decided beforehand, one of the secretaries spending an afternoon getting us to pick what we'd have, to speed things up, this was Christmas after all. It was easier not to talk with the food arriving and I showed a huge interest in everything Tommy Mooney had to say, we were lashing the wine too while Carrie Crowe played with her plate, flicking at the green starter like she was picking glass from a wound.

Morley made one or two attempts at conversation but thankfully he was ambushed by some of the juniors keen to hang on his every word so I was well through the steak before he leant across Carrie and touched my arm.

'How are you keeping Robbie?'

'I'm grand, grand. How are you ... ah, Trevor?' And I held my glass towards Tommy who'd begun to hum and seemed to be having difficulty focussing on the mouth of the glass.

'Steady it! Steady it!' He mumbled and he sloshed a little on my wrist as he poured.

'Robbie?' Morley again. He glanced quickly at Carrie who was thrashing something vegetarian into an even bigger looking mess, picking the large black beans from the wreckage and eating them.

'What?' I was drawn between the question and Tommy Mooney who was attempting to dye the sleeve of my good jacket a deep red. 'What?'

Morley hesitated; I could see he'd had a few. He glanced at Carrie again.

'Robbie, you know we're all a family. We care for each other. Deeply. I have broad shoulders ...'. He tilted his glass a little, took a sip. 'I'd like to lend you my shoulders. If there's anything we can do?'

'Do? About what?'

Tommy Mooney was mopping the tablecloth now and patting my arm, sloshing more wine from my glass. Morley hesitated again.

'If we can help in any way. Maybe a little time off?' He glanced at Carrie again. 'Or maybe counselling? The firm would gladly pay. We're a family after all. We do care'.

I could feel the room temperature falling.

'Counselling? For what?' Fucken Mooney knocked my glass again with the bottle, attempting to replace what he'd spilled.

'Maybe it's not the time?' Morley looked unsure and Carrie turned her full attention to him.

'Maybe not, Trevor'. She went back to digging for beans.

'Trevor? Well fuck me, there's a first!' And I was on my feet. Someone shouted SPEECH! And I could see Clancy laughing.

'G'wan Robbie'. He raised his pint. Morley had stood up too, his napkin in his outstretched hand.

'Fuck you!' I hissed. 'Fuck you, you ...'

Tommy Mooney was trying to mop my sleeve again and mumbling about waste so I emptied my full glass into his lap and turned back to Morley.

'You bollocks! You swing in here and get ahead of all of us, the big boss and now you want to counsel us? Well you know what you can do with your shoulders ...' I slapped down the napkin and stumbled across my chair. Tommy Mooney was dabbing at his crotch with his napkin and giggling, his eyes crinkled.

'You tell him Robbie. Good man!'

I had to get out but my feet were tangled so I grabbed the back of Carrie's chair. She shied away.

'Don't worry Crow; I wouldn't touch you with, with ... And those beans will only give you wind, but with that bollocks there you're probably well used to that already'. And I straightened my collar as best I could and found the door.

The taxi was quiet and my head was swimming, shadow estates racing by, the driver giving up early on any chance of conversation. Counselling? I must have drifted off because the next thing I remembered was the driver shaking my arm, and the low ticking of the engine.

'We're here sir. The bus-stop'. I focussed on the few trees, Cooley's new house.

'But I don't live here now'.

'This was the address you said sir, and it's twelve Euros'. He was in his thirties and stocky but I wasn't going to pay that and I told him. I'd get another taxi, I was living in town now and he could whistle for the twelve. I slipped from the car and started unsteadily down the shortcut, the driver slow to get his door open. Fuck him.

The blow sent me forward, the old wall of Tommy's garden looming and I hit the pebbledash hard and head-on, a flash of light and a hissing in my ears. I could feel his hands on me, ripping through my pockets as he searched for my wallet. I struggled and he hit me again, a solid wooden crack and then nothing.

I could smell clay and the rusted tang of blood; my hands were sticky with it. It was still dark and my suit was stiff with dew and I knew I'd pissed myself. The night was very still with that silence which whispers how late it is and the wine and Guinness churned in my gut as I attempted to stand. I was going to be sick and I tried to reach the wall as my stomach heaved. I met the wall again face first, the punch of it hitting me, the pain of it filling me with light as I smashed my head against it again, and then again.

Snowdrops

I've run away from very little since I left home, but in my mind I'm running now. Moving out wasn't a way of running either, but the old boy was a loser the first day ever and if you hang around that it can become a way of living too. So I moved out and I've moved on a few times since, sometimes with a woman and sometimes not, but I was settled now, without a woman as it happens, but you can't have everything.

I can't say that the vibe was in my head when I saw her for that first time with her tight jeans, a blazing sunrise on her arse pocket and a little floaty top. She was towing a wheelie case along the central traffic island, heading towards Jury's Hotel, the right side of thirty, and pretty with it, the sun shining down on all of us.

There was just something in the way she walked, it seemed like she loped, and with a fitness to her stride, even though the bag looked full, looked like all she had. Yes, it was like she loped, her cheap sunglasses reflecting my red van going by, reflecting all the buildings, all the other walking people too, the river running beyond us, the gulls crying up a storm, just like always.

I was trawling for a parking space that day. Somewhere close so I could sit for an hour or so, get a sandwich and a pint or if I met someone, maybe two pints and chat and forget about the work. She stopped and looked up at the face of the hotel and I thought 'tourist' or maybe 'student' but then again maybe 'worker' because we were a criss-cross map of workers, waitresses, and bar girls, temping staff and foragers, everyone searching for a niche, the next 'thing' big or not. I liked the way her heels clipped purposefully on the dry cement as she passed by, her glance in my direction just about visible above the plastic rims, a flicker, I thought, but I've seen a lot of flickers in my close to thirty years, so what?

I didn't exactly love wallpapering but I did it when I had to and I was out on the Western Distributor Road that week slapping paste on a landing and a couple of rooms, rose petals everywhere, turning a brand new box into somewhere I would have found it hard to live, the paper already closing in.

But Ellen lived alone and she paid well and early, and I could handle her standing too close and the constant cups of tea, the hovering and the perfume that matched the paper. 'Catwoman' my little sister would have cried but she wasn't here and there wasn't a cat that I could see. But maybe it was a virtual cat, cloying and close, its claws at the backdoor, its low meow crying in the air everywhere, its jagged scratchings on the stripped pine.

I had the sandwich finished and the pint well shot when she walked in, the case still looked heavy and she made not to see me but I offered her how warm it was to be towing anything and, with the counter empty, it got easy to talk.

Her accent wasn't Irish but her English was, the odd inflection we never hear ourselves use unless someone from outside uses it and maybe leans just a little too heavy on it here and there, like when I said my name was Shay and her 'how's it going' was pure Dublin but with another river running through it, maybe the Vistula or even the Dnieper, time would tell.

The job got pushed back again that afternoon. I had to ring Ellen with her waiting, dusty walls and say how the van had broken down right in the middle of Water Lane with nothing getting past, steam pouring out and a police car stuck behind me. I always give good detail in a lie. I learned that from the ould fella, he was a liar for years, good at it and handy with the detail, it makes it stand. Ellen was all 'Shay this' and 'Shay that'. She nearly offered to pay me more until she remembered that I was well ahead of schedule with the money and a bit behind with the paper and paste. But at least she swallowed it and how I'd have it fixed by tomorrow and how I'd get on to the landing before lunch.

Zlata didn't drink much but we still made an afternoon of it and, to be fair, my mates left me to it, Frankie coming in and catching my eye, his glance sweeping up to the mirror above the fireplace, his nod gone before it registered and I bought her another wine standing at the bar, our shoulders touching. She'd only left Dublin that morning, had been doing time as a barmaid in one of the grinder pubs in Temple Bar for about six months, all cockney stags and 'allo loves', manic weekends and the minimum wage if you were lucky, the tips disappearing down the manager's throat, the bouncers all poking fingers and rough hands.

The little house in St John's wasn't much, was hardly anything if you looked at it at all, but I'd rented it now for nearly three years when I got back from London, and held onto it after my last girlfriend left. It didn't break the bank and I'd kept it painted after a fashion and even if the floors creaked, the roof didn't leak and it was pleasant and cool in the summer when the rain kept off. The little backyard was a confusion of colourful weeds and a few of the shrubs I'd rescued from a garden 'refurb' in Rockbarton North the previous spring.

'What are they? The plants?' She'd asked after I'd carried her bag upstairs and we'd spent the evening on the low bed I called home and she'd pinned me to the mattress sitting astride my best effort, whispering urgent 'somethings' in her own language, her long hair flailing me, the drink running through us like familiarity.

'Don't really know', was the best I could manage, too relaxed and out of it to be up and checking and she'd stood there, her slim body with a halo around it as the sun went down and we'd made love again and hit the Róisín Dubh for some indie band trying to be the next big thing and missing it by a short mile at least.

Funny how your life can expand and it doesn't hurt at all. I've been there when love walked in, took a look at the rotting floorboards and the creaking underfoot, left a suitcase in the corner, dropped a coat across it, pulled up a chair and sat down, soothing that thing in your chest which you only recognise is a gap when the same love says 'that's it so', pushes the chair back, picks up an old coat and leaves.

But this wasn't like that at all, this was more of an accommodation for both of us, an address we shared easily over the growing weeks and the months. It kept each of us sane, even from that first morning and I'd left the spare key by the cooling kettle, the brush of her breasts still warm on my lucky face, my head around it all, for now at least.

I spread a lot of wallpaper that day even with Ellen and her cups of tea and her piercing gaze, standing behind me while I brushed and pasted, her perfume just a little close, the lonely pull of it clawing at me. I could feel the threatening purr, the presence of the cat, but I still skipped out the door that evening, my heart a butterfly, another 'fifty' in my old shirt, Ellen paying to please, and I got to the Italian place before it closed, bought enough for a pasta and ravioli dinner and two good reds.

She was in the backyard when I arrived, most of the weeds not just beaten back but gone, the wheelie-bin overflowing with shattered green, the soil black and broken up, 'ready for planting' as I put it, puffing out my gardening chest and Zlata laughed.

'Do you not like my hard work?' She pointed. 'Do you not like my flowerbed?' The raised hill of soil sloped up to the cement wall, a flat stone and some broken rubble set into it like steps and she picked the empty packs from the windowsill.

'I have planted these', she smiled. 'And we will have many flowers in the spring and snowdrops too'.

So she was staying and it registered inside me somewhere that this was ok, was good in fact and we set to cooking the ravioli and pasta, the wine open, sipping as we went. Every so often I would pause, the steam from the pan blurring the windowpane and look at the half-transformed garden, the weeds gone, the lank grasses no longer choking the leggy shrubs, little hills of soil around the roots and once she slipped her hand around my waist, joining me.

'I will finish it myself; you have your work to do'.

She was right, it got easier to face the wall, spread the paste on the flat paper, fold it over and layer it, carry the folds to the stepladder, fix the top line and drop it lightly into place, smooth out the creases and wipe away the excess, Ellen leaving me to it, knowing in some way that the game had moved on, knowing now that tea and perfume wouldn't do it. When it came for me to move Ellen passed me on to another friend with rooms to paint, a vein of work building out of the job completed well and I began to keep it easy and simple, the way I should.

The house in St John's was changing too, not so much chintzy or anything but tidier, cleaner, new cushions sitting easy on the old couch, our music collection building by the hi-fi I'd rescued from a Salthill skip, working perfectly, but obsolete in this time of mp3s and downloads. Even with the coming of the winter the garden held its shape, the shrubs bushier, the autumn leaves from next door's chestnut raked and stacked, decaying towards a mulch, the flowerbed bare but settled, a sharp peep of daffodil spear here and there through the dark soil.

Zlata would come from the garden pushing a strand from her smudged cheek, her fingers brown from the work and call me 'husband' and we would both laugh, not needing it. She took a two-day job at the weekends helping at the hairdressers around beside the church, the cash buying her the 'little extras' for the house, for both of us too, pictures framed and hung around the walls.

It wasn't the first night she bit me that led to the conversation. Sometimes at the height of things she'd nip my neck, sink her teeth in a little until one night, for fun, I pretended to collapse, slumping into the mattress, dead, and she stopped, sliding down the length of me, shaking my shoulders, calling, 'Shay, stop, stop, no messing'. I'd held it for fifteen seconds, which is a long time to be dead and then I jumped her and she screamed, probably disturbing the old couple next-door as I rolled her under me, her cries a mixture of fear and excitement.

'I thought you were dead'. She was on her back, the sheet around us, our eyes locked.

'You bit me', I laughed. 'You deserved a scare, you, you, vampire'.

'Vampire? They sleep in the dark. When I die I want to be, to be buried with lots of, of, flowers'.

'Flowers? You mean wreaths?'

'Yes, wreaths too, but flowers, how do you say it? Bouquets?'

'Ah, bouquets'.

'Yes and live flowers planted on my grave'.

I had to laugh; this conversation was spinning way off the beam.

'Planted?'

'Yes, every spring flowers would burst up, be bursting out of my body'.

'Bursting?'

'Yes, daffodils and tulips bursting out of my breasts, my navel, lots of little flowers. Yes, and snowdrops, a bunch of them to hold here, in my hands, like this and every spring they will burst up and hang their heads in pity for me, the tripping of the sun beginning again, this I want ...'

'And what will burst from here?' And I slipped my hand between her thighs, rolled on her again; her cries even louder than before.

The band was thumping out that old 80s tune 'Mirror in the Bathroom', the punters heaving, the bar three deep. The thin girl came out of the crowd, her face closed but her eyes on Zlata. I saw Zlata blink, then her eyes jumped to me, then away again to the girl and they spoke in their own language, moving away a little, the girl's hand on Zlata's sleeve.

I stuck with the band; they were locals, the crowd regular too. Every so often I'd glance towards the two girls their conversation animated, but then every nationality has its own way of talking. I've often seen Spaniards and

Italians wind-milling it on Shop Street, all screaming together, all cries and little gasps, loud hails and gestures to beat the band and very often it turns out to be nothing more than a lost glove or a misplaced hat, so who can tell?

Then Zlata shook her hand free and turned away, the other girl going as if to follow her but Zlata spun and faced her. I'd never seen Zlata angry in our few months together but she was angry now, her hands out, the nails pointed, her eyes blazing and the other girl backed away.

'What is her problem?'

'It is nothing; Kinga thinks I owe her money'.

'Money? How much?'

'I don't, I gave it to her boyfriend. She is, she is, as, how you say? Trying it on, yes, trying it on'.

And we left it at that. She was a little subdued on our way home and once I saw her glance into the shadows near the church as we passed, the evening gone quieter and astray.

Next day I was fencing a garden up on the Circular Road, enclosing a handkerchief of land behind latticed panels, driving stakes into the soft soil. The house owner was on a day off to help and tending to his few ridges, keen to talk about his composting and building up a 'tilth' as he called it, getting ready to feed his family from his own 'beds', not trusting the food he could buy at the supermarket, all herbicides and weed killers, his wife nodding in agreement.

'Lazy beds, that's what we call them', he smiled, loosening the soil. 'I'm growing our own potatoes, cabbage and carrots, the kids are all up for it, and we'll grow flowers as well, maybe bluebells and snowdrops'. And I thought of Zlata, how urgent her lovemaking had been once we'd reached home the night before, how it had surprised me, the way she'd held me, her mumbled gasps as she came, her eyes glassy and full in the low light.

The knocking on the door came not long after I got home, my hands still black from the creosote. I thought Zlata had forgotten her key calling 'hold on love' as I fiddled with the lock but it was some charity worker asking if he could collect the bag of clothes, how Zlata had taken the bag some days before and asked him to call back.

I took the stairs in two's but there was no bag, in fact there was nothing at all, Zlata's clothes were gone, her one heavy bag was gone, the drawers empty, the charity guy bemused as I sent him away. I wandered around to the hairdressers where she worked, but it was closed and when I rang the phone number stencilled on the window I could hear the phone ringing out in the darkened shop.

It's easier than we think to disappear; anyone can do it. I knew her name, I suppose I did, but did I? So I waited, hung around the Róisín, maybe her thin-faced friend would come in, but she didn't, so we move on, we make do, we work or not. Love had picked up that old coat and left. I shook my head when I called it love, it took me a little while to give it a name and it felt strange.

It was March and the wind off the river would peel paint, the gulls hanging above the tied-up fishing boats in the bouncing dock, the phone lines crying for want of a voice. I was moving a load of furniture when I saw Kinga again. I didn't expect it at all, my heart not in it but when she skipped down the steps of a cheap, day-by-day hotel near the railway station I swung the van and called her.

She didn't have a clue who I was, her eyes darting beyond me like she thought I was the police, her face even thinner than I remembered, the slicing wind from the river peeling tears from our eyes and she didn't want to talk but in the end I said 'please' and we went for a coffee and she told me.

'She is gone'.

'Gone? Yes I know that, but why?'

'She is gone. I know this; she has moved on, there is a reason. But you do not know? How could you?' She fumbled and hummed but in the end she settled, told me the story, how Zlata had come here with her boyfriend, how much she loved him, how he was a boxer, how 'brutal' he was to her, her word, then she stopped and looked at me again.

'He beat her every time. We all saw it'.

Then her boyfriend was killed at their house in Blanchardstown; he was stabbed.

'She has moved on now, because I saw her. She is afraid I will say'.

I'm standing at the bathroom mirror, and I've never run from anything before but I'm considering it now. There's a watery sun fracturing the window glass and I'm scraping at yesterday's beard with a blunt blade. I can see in the light the way her bulbs are budding, bursting through the soil and I can hear Kinga's voice telling me again how the boyfriend died. Telling me how many times he was stabbed, how when the police came to the house the corpse was spread-eagled, in his own blood, the bed black with it.

How his hands were gone, his boxer's hands, no trace of them was ever found and in the watery light I can see the raised flowerbed against the block wall and I remember. The miniature daffodils are bending in the breeze, the single, small cupped bunch of snowdrops at the very centre, their bell-like flowers barely open but hanging their heads in pity, their outer petals closed, the leaves twitching like narrow green blades.

FLOORED

The day we moved in Gerry started with the nail gun almost immediately, spreading the heavy membrane and laying out the polished boards in vertical stacks. The metallic clack-clack as the sharpened spikes gripped them to the wooden joists filled the shell of the house, the clack-clack shooting through us all, pinning us too, hemming us in, me and the children, the baby restless, Bronagh staring at the TV screen following Peppa Pig on her travels. The clack, clack echoed off the bare walls, the baby twitching to it in her sleep and Gerry covered in sawdust and shavings, ploughing through the house like an angry squall, short with all of us.

'That fucker Corrigan's bailed out'. I can still remember that day in Manchester when Gerry came home early from the site, the flats half up, labourers like insects crawling over everything and Gerry had just heard how Corrigan had sold it on as a going concern except the new developer had his own sub-contractors and Gerry was out. We'd packed what we could and vanished, me out to here with the baby. Bronagh was only two and Gerry had just emptied our bank accounts, paid no one and we were on the evening ferry by the time his men learned that he wasn't coming back from ordering plasterboard and battens, that their wages would be staying unpaid.

But we got over it even if the running name followed us. I'd have been happy in a one-roomed flat in Manchester, a bedroom and a cubbyhole toilet and 'fuck-off' neighbours too, but Gerry always wanted more so he'd even sold the digger over the phone cheap to a friend while we were racing for the boat.

The Griffins had rescued us, ready to build a house when we arrived. Gerry had priced it well and that was the start. Then he bought a site from Christy Convoy, got it handy and maybe we should have wondered why but it looked like a chance and we had to, so we took it.

'We'll be moving in on Friday'. That was how he put it. I was holding down a shift and a half at the local Supervalu just to keep the food flowing. Gerry's mother was minding Bronagh and the baby, so moving all our stuff out of the home house and into a half-finished shell was the last thing I needed, hiking black sacks up newly-nailed stairs, no banisters and Bronagh balanced on the edge looking down, Gerry screaming 'don't move Bronagh, don't move' his arm outstretched, his fingers splayed.

I'd never been able to figure out why old Tommy Walshe got so upset about us building the house. We bought the site fair and paid for it too. He came after Gerry like he was a thief, accusing him of taking what wasn't rightfully his. I heard Gerry shouting that day he chalked the site, the digger ripping in and Gerry telling the old man to 'fuck off' his fist raised and old Tommy Walshe had brushed past me as I pushed the pram, Bronagh fast asleep, his eyes burning into the two of us, like we shouldn't be there.

'What's the matter with him?' That was all I said and Gerry had exploded, cursing at the old ways, shouting how times were changing and how he was sick of 'ould fuckers' like Tommy Walsh holding the country back and Gerry started in, day and night, wet and dry, putting blocks on top of each other because he had to, particularly after Tommy Walsh died.

Afterwards I would come to see how Gerry had it almost all worked out, maybe even without knowing it. With the roof on and all the windows in place, the plasterers and electricians had swarmed over the shell like fat flies cleaning out a carcass. Except they were stitching things into place, cables and pipes and wires and switches, lengths of timber, angles of doors and skirtings and the house grew like one of those time-lapse photography shows on the Discovery channel. Gerry watched it all fill and breathe, flex and grow muscle until it was almost ready and he knew, standing before it one summer's evening, the sun burning off the new plaster that the money was so tight that he'd have to move in and finish it off himself.

The first time he hit Bronagh I didn't speak to him for two days. Slipping off the edge of his half-floored bedroom was easy for a three-year old, as she ran to him to show her newest picture and how the family, our family, could be picked out around the box she'd drawn and I'd written 'Our House' in big print over the top of it. I heard her wails coming back to the kitchen, carrying, as her little legs clattered, Gerry cursing after her, his face red with anger, the red tracks of his hand already raised on her pale legs.

'For fuck's sake Gillian, she nearly went into the floor space!' We screamed each other out then, spit and venom and I'd taunted him with Manchester and how he was such a small man. He'd pulled his arm back and I'd dared him to hit me until the baby started to gag on the full spoon and he'd stalked away.

'I'll be going back to England in a few weeks'. That was how he put it to me on the Thursday, refusing to meet my eyes.

'Oh?'

'It's for the best, the money's better and I'll do six months, and we'll be able to finish here'. And that had thawed us a little bit and he'd hugged Bronagh, but when he came to me that night smelling of sweat and resin, his hands calloused on my breasts, his mouth hungry on my neck, driving hard into me, his breathing fast and ragged and he'd whispered 'I love you' as we'd fucked, I had denied it for him saying, 'no you don't' and he'd pulled out of me, still hard and rolled on his back and sighed and slept.

Sometimes now I stand at the corner of the sunroom when the light is good and I look towards the corner where old Tommy Walshe had lain that night he killed himself. The police had taken the body away, leaving the sodden grave, his blood mixed into the soil, the land black with it, then they took the picture he'd pinned to his chest, 'Angelground' scrawled across it and questioned Gerry about what it meant, as if he could know and he'd shaken his head and drained his cup and said nothing.

It wasn't long after that until Mullins, the big auctioneer, called and said how the O'Rourkes were no longer interested in buying the house but that he'd keep it on his books. Houses were flying out the door and the boom would run forever, he smiled, his new Lexus gleaming in the lane.

But ours didn't grow wings, not that we didn't have people interested but it was like word spread almost without the need for words. I saw it myself, couples dashing towards the half-finished pile, their arms outstretched, the wife looking back at the husband nodding, and yet within a week the word would come back that they'd found something better.

When a letter comes I take it down to Gerry's mother to read. His brother Martin has no interest, just farming, a singular man he observes me, that's the best way I can describe it, his world is all inside, like London is another galaxy so I read her the letter, emphasising the best bits, filling in where he's doing well. I knew at some stage I had to let her know how he isn't coming back, how he's met this Dutch woman and how he's happy that I keep the house just to get me out of his hair. But I still keep it simple, her sight's failing now so I skim over it and the girls lean in on her aproned lap and smile up into her vague stare.

It was later on I found out how old Tommy Walshe had thought he' d given the site to the Council as a monument, a little park. The blocks were well up the day I wheeled the baby along the laneway to the back of the site, Gerry making sure that the line was changed, filling in the spot where Tommy had died and extending the curtain wall beyond it, his 'grave' filled in, all his shadows buried, the new wall enclosing everything.

'Have you no shame?' She asked, this middle-aged woman who stalked from the locked-up remains of Tommy's house, a young girl following her, holding her arm. 'Have you no shame at all?'

And what could I do but face her, asking her to explain her anger. So she told me everything, even everything Gerry didn't know: how Tommy was her father, how he had family buried there from years before. How the Church wouldn't take the un-baptised ones, the lost infants, the buried ones, how they'd driven him at some level even he didn't understand, caretaker, undertaker, father, gaoler, guard.

'He thought we never knew about them'. She mocked, 'but which mother wouldn't trust her daughters, which mother doesn't share?' She turned to hug her own daughter, a teenager, all gangly and wide eyed who tried to pull her away.

And I told it all to Gerry, explaining at last what had come to what, why old Tommy had called it Angelground, how things were and he'd shook his head the way men do and said it couldn't be helped, not now anyway.

After that I couldn't hide. What we'd done was done. Gerry said the old ways were gone. The nail gun punching the spikes home, slating the subfloor over, laying down a new veneer, Bronagh running across it, the baby crawling, and Gerry hurrying to get it finished, only the sunroom and the back bedroom left to go.

'I'm fucken' stretched, Gillian, will you give me a hand?' He stood in the door of the living room, his eyes red from sawdust, his jaws unshaven and I knew he was asking. I suppose being a couple comes down to that, holding things behind your ribs, rebuilding on scarred foundations and praying nothing happens to cause too big a crack in the whole thing.

And so I'd gone on my knees in the sunroom and set the boards for him, unrolling the heavy plastic, spreading the membrane tight, turning the subfloor opaque, muffling the cement smell and Gerry slipped the boards into place, locking them together before the clack, clack of the nail gun clamped them, the short nipple pressed into the wood and the trigger pulled, the jump of the gun, the spikes sinking in, down to the wedged head, the boards sighing almost, as he pressed and shot, pressed and shot.

'I'm running it close'. Gerry confessed on the Friday morning, the small bedroom still to go and the ferry to catch from Dublin on the Friday night, so we'd put our backs into it sheeting and stapling the small space,

Bronagh on Peppa watch, the baby sleeping and I suppose it was the wrong time to open up wounds again.

We were planning visits while we worked, the clack, clack of the nail gun bouncing off the walls, Gerry bent close to the pinned boards. I was still holding out for a September visit and then he'd be home for Christmas.

'Maybe you could come over in August and again in November, I'll be on good money and saving hard'. He'd got a chance of a job in London with the McCulloughs, he'd worked for them before and they paid well. But I was holding out for September and then for Christmas to bring him home.

'I might not be finishing up at Christmas', was all he said and then we were rowing again, our voices raised, me accusing him of planning this behind my back. How I'd heard him on the phone to McCullough's foreman talking about two years and how he'd promised me he'd only do six months.

Bronagh came to the door, her eyes flooding as she looked at us there astride the half-finished floor and he roared at her to go and she ran from the room, her sobs carrying to us off the bare walls.

'You're some bastard!' I was raging and he swung, his open hand catching me along the cheek, my spit flying.

I sat in the cold kitchen Bronagh on my knee, ignoring the hammering, the punching of the nails, and the rattle of the gun as he finished out the last room. I'd had enough of this, there would have to be some change, we could not continue like this, there was no future, no light.

'I'm short a bale of boards'. He stood at the kitchen door. 'I'll get them from the shed and say goodbye to the mother and Martin at the same time'.

I said nothing, holding Bronagh closer, and the baby crawling towards him on the rug so he turned and clattered from the house banging the door behind him. We were still there, the children bothering my time, when he got back and he stood at the door casually after carting a bail of timber along the corridor.

'The mother said to leave the children down about five. I've said my goodbyes'. And he'd gone back to the work while I readied their meals, sealing dishes and packing changes of clothes. I'd be back late from the ferry and I'd have to collect the children in the morning. This was a big adventure staying with granny and Bronagh ran packing her favourite books, her crayons, her beloved Peppa, the baby's bits.

When he bent to hug the baby I thought I'd cry but I held it in, my face still tight, my eye bloodshot and when his mother took the baby in her arms she'd touched my arm, her gaze resting on the bruise.

'He's had no luck since buying that place', was all she said and I'd driven the short journey home thinking how she was probably right, but knowing he'd had a choice, we'd both had a choice, but there was nothing to do about it now.

I stood at the bedroom door, Gerry had about a few dozen boards to go, pinning the plastic as he went.

'Did you deliver them?'

I nodded yes. He held my stare. 'Good, it's for the best then; I'll be ready here and pack a bag'.

He struggled with the sheeting. I knew he wouldn't let things go. 'You don't love me anyway. I'm as well off'.

I knew then he wouldn't be back, he'd meet someone and that would be an end to it. She'd have his children and I would be left. It was so unfair and I watched as he slipped the last of the plastic into place, cut the roll and knelt to put the next polished board in place, his hand scrabbling behind him for the nail gun.

'Here'. Was all I said, lifting it and pressing it to his skull, the clack, clack of the trigger pulled, the short nipple sinking in as he groaned once the steel pin travelling upwards into his brain, the second one following close behind.

There was hardly any blood, I had two hours to wrap him in the plastic, sealing it before I eased him into the floor space and stapled the membrane into place, the subfloor opaque, his face misted already through the wrap, blurring his body forever. The remaining boards slotted easily, the nail gun pinning them, the beading slipping into place and I was ready to drive to the ferry port with time to spare. I even waved to the departing boat, picked out some polite, unknown man waving back, blew him a kiss even, which I thought was nice, then I drove home.

We seldom go into the backroom now. I use it as a storeroom. Broken furniture and old chairs, Gerry's mother has been good to us, better since I told her about the Dutch woman. Once a year he sends a card, the girls love to get it. I always manage to get it posted, sometimes in London, or Newcastle, Cardiff even, he moves around a lot and about three times a year I write a letter in the same black inked scrawl he always used, no one asks, no one notices, they feel sorry for us being abandoned like this, for me having to work, and at night if I hear movement in the walls or down underneath I talk to old Tommy's shadows and tell them to be quiet.

What's Not Said

Spotter knew he was nervous when he found himself talking. He hated that because then he knew he was nervous, or keyed up, or whatever. He couldn't give a truepenny fuck about Manchester United and here he was jabbering on to some mad man with oily hair and three pints stacked before him and it wasn't even eleven yet.

'Keane was the man I tell you, a warrior!' The oily one roared, heads turning in the crowded bar, eyes blanking but taking it all in, the pub band torturing a tune and the punters at the same time. Fuck Keane he felt like saying but he couldn't, he'd started the chat in the first place and now he was trapped. He needed to get to the car and just count the money again but he'd started chatting and the guy was still blowing on about the 2003 season. Fuck!

He thought of the money, five thousand, not a huge bet but substantial never-the-less, a lot of scraping to get it gathered, months, and 10/1 would make it a whole lot healthier. A lot healthier, guaranteed.

When Kingspin came in and Spotter collected his winnings he would change the car, not that the Red Beast was looking her age or anything but he'd love something with more 'go'. The Beast could still pull the young ones and their mothers too. Women fancied the red Merc with the classy alloys and the big fuckoff spoiler nailed to the boot lid. He'd picked it up in Liverpool that time he'd had the big win at Aintree. It looked like a drug king's car with all the extras, sleek and well finished and he'd just driven it on to the ferry and sorted the tax when he got home. Pity the looks didn't run to the engine, fucking diesel, no turbo just that sewing-machine rattle that'd do yer head and he was getting overtaken by milk floats.

He'd been up before six, bucket out, a gentle wax and never forget the alloys, and then the inside, carpets, dash and upholstery, sweat dripping off him, the tracksuit smelling, but he'd get the returns. He smiled again when he thought of his last trip to the Galway Races, three years back now. He was a businessman that year because you could be anything for a week, like stepping off the map, good suit and the bets were flying.

The German woman had been impressed, he'd just chatted her up in the queue, waiting to collect on another bet, the notes sprouting from his clenched fist like rich, golden leaves. Silke, he'd learned to say it with two syllables, Silk-e, she was over from Munich, something to do with grooming horses, blonde and big and happy to have a drink, her eyes on him.

Champagne in the owners and trainers tent, she loved it and three more winners after that. God that had been good. When he'd told Howley they'd almost pissed themselves.

'I couldn't lose. I was afraid to go for a piss in case I turned 'the lad' to gold when I touched it'.

Howley had laughed at that too. 'Yeah, fucking Golden Bollocks, that's you all right'.

They'd headed back to the city after that for a meal, Spotter trying to swing it towards Silk-e's hotel. When he was on his own and working, and betting was work, he usually slept in the car himself. He'd park up in a good hotel, get to the bar early, have a good steak and spend the night there, ear to the tipsters and a good cigar, say as little as possible and remember he was working. Later he'd remove the suit and fold it, stretch out along the back seat, roll in the blanket, best price and as the ball bounced that night he didn't need a hotel at all.

After the meal they'd set off along the teeming streets before easing on to the quieter side streets away from the main drag to find the Beast abandoned in some car park along the canals behind the Cathedral. He loved that building, reminded him of himself, pretending to be something it wasn't, barely built thirty years but pretending to have been there forever, yeah, he liked that.

But Silk-e couldn't wait, pulling him in some doorway by the river, her knee in his crotch, pushing against him, locked and hungry and he'd lost it himself, spinning her against the heavy door and she'd slipped down on one knee until the house lights had flared and they had to run and running wasn't the easiest for him bent over as he was with her hat held firmly in place to hide his stiffness and Silk-e turned, her throaty laugh carrying along the empty street, her high heels clipping.

The Beast had seen it all, young and not so, married and not, but he still smiled at the memory of the horny bonnet fuck, her arse slapping on the shine of the red paintwork, the car park hushed, the shadow of the Cathedral falling on them, his good suit trousers around his ankles, his shirt undone, her nails in his chest hair while she wore nothing but that hat, urging him on in his shortening strokes, still way faster than the church bell tolling midnight.

Yes, Eamonn still came to him, but not as badly now, not nearly so bad. Bloodied and broken, his eyes almost closed and Spotter working on his bones, moulding him, smoothing his bruises, struggling to stop the red flow, bringing life to his loose limbs, slapping his numb cheeks, peeling back his lifeless lids, blowing breath through his numbed lips.

It was supposed to be another easy one, the bare-knuckle fight out beyond the suburbs towards the north, the barn a regular venue, well wide of the city.

'He's supposed to be a handy one. Warness they call him, I asked around'.

That was how Tommy-T had put it and Tommy arranged all the fights, he did other stuff as well but Spotter never bothered with any of that, not his problem. 'You'll handle him though'.

Eamonn had nodded and Spotter had set him to the training, the gym work to bring him up, tone him, not that Eamonn needed a lot, the everyday grind nearly enough to keep him sharp.

'He's English, they say, Warness?' Eamonn had smiled, a sheen on his heavy shoulders, wiping the sweat from his face.

'He'll bleed like the rest of us, won't he?' Spotter had told him. 'And Tommy usually sets them well'.

Eamonn had said nothing, just gone back to the heavy battered bag swinging from the rafters of Spotter's shed, the weights laid out in rows, the mingled smell of sweat and hay.

Afterwards Tommy-T had cried worse than most, blaming himself for not checking further. At the funeral he'd stood well back from the grave, his head almost resting on his chest, tears streaking his heavy, stubbled cheeks.

'The Dublin lads said he was fine'. Was all he said and Spotter had shaken his hand telling him that there was no blame.

Spotter had won big in the past on Eamonn's fast hands, cutting down bigger men, taking their best and coming back, putting them down and putting them out. Sometimes it took an hour, no real rounds, Spotter acting as Eamonn's referee, the other man the same, with the refs agreeing all beforehand. It had been the same for years, no low blows, no biting, no heads, and Spotter had minded him well.

They'd been friends since school, not that Eamonn went there much except when the police insisted. Funny how Spotter had saved him from a beating once, he was smaller then, one of the Fahy's using the boot until Spotter had stepped in, the circle swaying across the gravelled schoolyard and he'd battered Fahy until Mr Noone had pushed through the crowd and ripped them apart.

'Thanks'. That was all Eamonn had said once the crowd had cleared and he was pushing at the streaked snot with his fists. Over the years that followed that had grown to a closeness and Spotter had become his second, even sparring with Eamonn but not in his league, the heavy gloves saving him. Eamonn would come to his house and they'd strap the gloves on circling around each other in the old barn. Spotter came to know his 'big' punch, the one extra move that all good fighters had. Eamonn would faint a left, his shoulder dropping for the throw but when Spotter moved to counter, Eamonn's right would already be tapping him on the chin and Eamonn would smile.

'Had you there Spot'. And Spotter would know that in real time he would be sleeping in Noddyland, all tucked in, all laid out, if Eamonn had put his weight behind the punch. Yes, sometimes it took an hour, both men eyes shut and shuffling but Eamonn's heart always held out, always.

Tommy-T always tried to set it well, Spotter knew this and they'd all taken money on Eamonn's fists, the weights were always close and the levels fair, sometimes Tommy's men were bigger and slower, Eamonn the whippet then, it balanced out. Eamonn had taken big money on bog roads and empty sheds, city centre car parks and back roads, hard men in tight bunches urging blood and pain, blood in their hearts, blood in their eyes.

Warness was different. He looked light, thin and undernourished almost, but there was something in the way he moved, like he wasn't really there at all, a wraith shifting, Eamonn's punches missing him, his missing little. Afterwards it was said how he was ex-army, trained to the pain, that Tommy-T had fucked it up, got it wrong and God, he had been hard, hard. Spotter shivered still. Twenty minutes in and Eamonn was in ribbons, cut up and battered but climbing off the torn ground, Warness beating him to everything, even his 'big' punch going wide, but fists up, too brave to stay down, Spotter pleading in his ear, Tommy-T as well.

Spotter still woke crying to the punch that did it, Eamonn's dance all broken and out of tune, his feet finding unseen footholds, shadow steps, his arms flailing, knuckles broken, his lips loose. Spotter was there to catch him, breathing him life, but he was already gone, down and dead and the crowd melting away, gone in no time, every man marked in some way by what they'd seen.

Tommy-T had left him at the hospital doors and the police had brought the body home and later they'd called to Spotter's home, Spotter standing by the farmhouse door, feigning ignorance with his heart broken and Eamonn dead.

'You trained him?' Howley was one of the old detectives, overweight and shrewd, knew stories going back thirty years, had seen mysteries, both solved and still mysterious and he knew the story well. Spotter had nodded.

'Yes we boxed a few rounds now and again'.

Howley had shaken his head at the end, knowing that Spotter would never talk. His friend was dead and that was that.

'I'm sorry', was all he said, the younger detective with him all keen for an arrest, Howley telling him to wise up, to leave it. 'Accidents will always happen'.

Spotter had drowned in Eamonn's blood, down in the piss pools and the vomit, the Red Beast up on blocks, the few fields left untended, the animals sold, and his winnings turning to amber gold in his open throat. Tears and women, good women, not new, but women who held him and loved him and drank his money and left him then, his money gone 'til the gutter carried him ashore and he was spent.

The smell brought him up short, a fly buzzing and the awful stench, sweat and drink, shit and stale urine, the ripeness filling his mind and he vomited again and he knew it was his own smell and he was down.

Howley saved him. A policeman and all that but hauling him into the police car and digging him out one last time, cutting off his crusted suit, peeling the socks from his blackened feet, forcing food into him with the booze, helping him to wash and shave, no, shaving him because his hands shook too much and he cried and watched Eamonn die again and then again, his cries waking the dead.

A month in Howley's back room and his darkness hung around him sighing, the buzz in his head, not dead but nowhere, barely alive until the day Howley took him shivering and sat him on the cracked doorstep in the warm sun and put the carton of cold milk in his unsteady hand and made him drink, its coldness cutting channels in his knotted gut. But he kept it down, tears in his eyes and he looked at the waxed carton and drank again.

'Why?' He'd faced Howley one day in the narrow kitchen and Howley had looked embarrassed and went to turn away.

'No. Why?' He raised his voice and Howley had smiled.

'Because there's very little black and white, I've learned that. And, maybe you had it earned'. And he'd smiled again and shook his head and they'd left it at that, knowing that what isn't said is often the reason for a lot that happens.

Spotter could still remember his first bet, the first bet of his second life. He won seven euros and some change and the girl brought his winnings to the table where he sat with Howley and the straining, wasp-thin greyhounds circled in the cold, white light.

They never spoke about Eamonn, not really, they sidled up to it a few times but it was Howley who appeared the more reluctant so Spotter had let it go. But that night at the dogs when Tommy-T had pushed through the crowds towards them Spotter had felt the chill coming off Howley; how his policeman's shadow had grown around him in the pushing bar and he'd become a stranger to Spotter, and Tommy-T had lowered his eyes for just a second before nodding to Howley and extending his pudgy hand to Spotter, his mumbled 'good to see you', taking Spotter by surprise.

'You're not a fan of Tommy then?'

Howley had taken Spotter's question well.

'No. I know him too well. I've seen what he can do. I know a lot he's done, I have my doubts. Can we leave it at that?

And now Spotter was back, two years gone and a good friend lost, but he was back. He'd loaded the Red Beast that morning after he'd showered, the land leased and the farmhouse cleaned, the ashes in the garden. The new suit was the best he could afford; the shirt was white and the five thousand, hard earned and scraped, in the cheap money belt, close to his pale flesh. He'd heard that Kingspin was lengthening, the odds out to tens, he'd been hoping for sevens and there it was, tens and maybe more and he was nervous again.

Burn

We were out for a burn in a stolen Ford. There was Bennie and me and Piedog in the back and we were high on a mixture of cider and beer and cheap coke, helping ourselves to Piedog's stash which he was supposed to be selling for his cousin Tommy-T but we were cutting it and cutting it and if we didn't stop soon we'd be down to pure starch.

I'd helped Bennie to pop the steering lock, the column giving with the force of an uppercut and he'd rummaged in the innards, his cheek against the dash and brushed the bare wires. The engine coughed a fluttering rasp and Piedog jumped in with the rattle of cans. He punched three and passed two of them over and we swung the car easy out of Holly Grove, onto Fuchsia, through the main road and off it to the roundabout at the college and clear. We sent the Ford hurtling along the Coast Road, the car swaying and skipping before swinging up the feeder road and bursting onto the motorway, coming at the Crescent through the new estates, full of Africans, full of Poles. We raced along the motorway, weaving through the other punters, the tyres humming on the white lines.

'We're going up the Crescent', Bennie cried, tearing the engine. 'Third ya fucker, third!'

And I found the gear. We often drove like this for the fun, half a driver each, Bennie on the clutch and me flicking through the gears. One night, eighteen months or so back, when we were all barely eighteen we robbed an old Volvo and the three of us had scrunched onto the wide front seats, Piedog on the brakes and clutch, Bennie on the steering and accelerator and me on the gears.

We made laps of the Crescent that evening and over into the New Park, all the houses glowing in the rich sun, the cheap estate looking like more than it really was, box houses for cardboard people, thrown up for us and our likes. We were brushing the walls and the girls all came out, calling to us, the summer evening full on. Even the mothers hung from the upstairs windows and urged us to go faster, Bennie steering closer and closer to the parked cars, climbing on the footpath here and there to send the little kids scrambling. We had the windows full down and as we drove we screamed, 'c'mon ye little fuckers', the kids up for the chase, their baby legs scrambling through the garden gates, their cheap sandals flashing as we scraped the pebbledash, paint and chips hitting the windscreen.

Someone phoned the cops in the end and we were on Clareview, chatting to Shelley and Claire Ann sitting on a front wall, Bennie screaming. 'Show us yer tits! Show us yer tits!' And Shelley all up for it when Piedog's strangled 'Cops!' made us look and the paddy wagon swung around from The Glebe and we were off.

'A fucking Transit!' Bennie laughed. 'Like they'll catch us in that', and he ran the Volvo two wheels up along the footpath and Shelley raised her top, her jelly tits wobbling at the van, the cops all sitting with their batons drawn.

I suppose I'm making that bit about the batons up but Piedog said it laughing:

'That'll stiffen their batons'.

Sweat trickled into the folds of his neck fat as he looked back, giving them the finger, laughing. He was working on this slicked-down blade job, the hair thick with wax, pulling it into little blade points of hair stuck in a short fringe across his freckled forehead. He was letting it grow after his last fight, said it made him look tougher when he fought; he was the fighter in the family now, bare knuckle. We'd been there watching him cut the Mullingar lad down in ten minutes but he still had bruises so he was growing the hair again and we didn't care because we'd cleared five hundred on the fight, money for jam.

He was giving the fingers to the cops, three of them sitting in the front seat, their faces set and their three uniforms looking like one giant uniform, supercop in a Transit van, their police caps already on. They were giving us the hard stare even though the Transit was labouring, the Volvo pulling away, fucking them off.

Bennie had taken over all the driving now, wanting to keep ahead when a second carload of cops swung out of Rocklands to cut us off and Bennie never blinked, catching them with the wing of the Volvo, a puff of rust and one wiper blade flying up across the windscreen, the police car slewing around, the driver winding the wheel, his mouth open, swearing like he was spinning on ice.

'Fuckers!' Piedog pulled his hoodie up and we all did the same, didn't need to advertise ourselves, even though they knew us well. Both police wagons slotted in behind us as Bennie took us around again, sweeping past Shelley and Claire Ann, both of them with their t-shirts raised, breasts jiggling, the police, face front, the Transit screaming as the driver stretched the gears.

'Head for the funnel!' I pointed, even though Bennie knew the laneway well, the police car ahead of the Transit now and trying to get level. We hit the narrow path between The Glebe and Castle Road and Bennie hit the brakes, the police car on our bumper because the driver knew that the path narrowed at the very end, we could get the front doors open as Bennie put the tail in the wall, the rake of metal, the crunch of toughened glass. He cut the engine and tossed the keys and that was that, we were well gone and hiding before the cops even got around the Volvo jammed between the narrow walls.

But there would be none of that this evening. Bennie was on the lookout, I could feel it. He kept scanning out the windows as we tooled along, the Ford purring, all of us buzzing as well, Piedog cracking tins and doling out the odd snort. Every so often he'd mutter,

'Fuck it, Tommy'l never cop it'. And he'd opened another wrap and shared the powder out and then he stored the little slip of silver paper carefully in his t-shirt pocket. He'd re-cut what remained in his stash when we got back down to the house.

Bennie was boiling too, we'd have to be careful, he'd gotten moody in the past while and even though we could guess what was bothering him, he'd only say when he'd say. He'd caught me by the throat a week back outside the Spar when I asked something, his eyes like fire points, shining under the black cap, his stubble smeared with crumbs and he'd mashed the leftovers of the sausage roll into my face.

'Fuck off Dessie and don't be a cunt!' And it had only been some stupid question about a girl or something, did he fancy her, so I was always careful now and with Piedog supplying, Bennie was on a rush.

'Where does Stanners live?'

I saw Piedog give him a look, staring at the back of his scrawny neck as he brushed by a Corolla, baring his teeth at the woman driver.

'The can guy?'

'Yeah, that little fucker, spraying his tags everywhere. He should stick to his own side'.

I met Piedog's eye, Bennie glancing in the mirror.

'Fucker! Fucker! Fucker!' He was pounding the steering wheel with his left hand and I was waiting for the airbag to pop but it didn't. Bennie caught Piedog's eye again.

'Didya see it?' And Piedog nodded.

'Yeah, we both did. Stanners, he's still only a prick, taggin' everything'. Piedog was being careful. I could feel it even over the buzz, my heart racing, but I agreed.

'Yeah we saw it'.

But Bennie was ignoring us again, scanning down the narrow offshoots, hoping to see something; we didn't know what, his head wheeling, the Focus chugging in second.

'He lives around here, doesn't he?' And we nodded, I knew Stanners from the clubs, a little skinny guy with four tops and a puffa jacket to make up bulk and always with a spray can and he'd tag anything, busses, walls, parked trucks. Story was he'd tagged a taxi once, in the line, with the driver in it.

And now he'd tagged Bennie, 'Bennie Sucks Cock' in his favourite powder blue, the letters meshed and leaning into each other, every letter loving the one next to it, hugging it, and his signal STNR there beside it, the letters all entwined, like snakes, easing around each other, hooked, the blue sinking into the blocks of the wall of the back way to the shops where we cracked our cans sometimes when we were bored.

'There!' Piedog pointed and Bennie swung the Ford down a narrow side street but it was only a teenager in a big jacket and Bennie swung in beside him, eyeing him, the kid pretending blindness, not liking the smell of the car, not liking the look of us.

'Hey! Fuckface! Where does Stanners live?' But the kid kept walking like he was deaf, which was sure to wind Bennie up.

'Hey! Hey!' Bennie hit the brakes and he was out, crossing the path, the car still rolling and I grabbed the handbrake, He pinned the kid down over the low garden wall, his face inches from the kid's.

'You deaf? I'm looking for Stanners. The can guy?!'

'Fuck off willya, he lives down there'. He pointed in the general direction of the church and Bennie gave him a smack on the head and threatened a second before he jumped back in and I slipped the handbrake again. Piedog popped us two more cans and Bennie went back to muttering, trying to make eye contact with anyone driving or walking as we turned down towards the grey church, an old lady dipping her fingers in the water font, all the doors locked in case anyone robbed the empty poor-box.

Bennie was really getting wound up now, we all were, and Piedog was squinting out the back window and swigging a can. He was fidgeting too, hoping that Stanners would pop up out of the ground, a big fucking blue can in his hand, a big blue arrow in the sky above him and we could corner him and kick him shitless and go home and finish the cans or sell a few wraps to the dopers down behind the centre and give the grease to Piedog's cousin Tommy-T and take our cut.

Bennie started to swear, swigging the can and swearing, cursing Stanners to death. I'd seen him like this but lately he was getting worse, we'd better find him and soon or

Piedog and myself would be bailing out, moving car or not and taking to the back lanes, hoping he'd quiet down.

I never saw the knife until he sunk it into the dashboard, ripping it again and again, fucking it in there, bits of foam and plastic flying up, Bennie's spits flying.

'Try the funnel, I saw him once around the shops'. I hadn't but we should try there and I had to say anything to keep him moving, and I pointed.

'Swing down The Glebe'. I could feel my heart pumping, the burn of the coke in behind my eyes, my nostrils like frosty air with little icy things floating in it, my heart like some big drum, the loud thump, thump of it, but he did it, muttering. 'Yeah, the shops, the shops, the shops'.

And we were sweeping along past Rockfield, past Shelley's house but she didn't live there since the kid, past Claire Ann's, she was with some foreign guy now over on the west side and thinned down to nothing.

Bennie had the knife in his lap and was back drumming the steering wheel, muttering again, and he swung the wheel and sent us shooting down the funnel, the walls closing in beside us and then he slowed and then he slowed and then he stopped.

'Wha?' And we followed as he pointed. The tag was at least two feet high and blue, the bluest blue, Stanners blue and Bennie's face was frozen, and there was a drawing this time, my little brother, if I had one, could probably have done better, but it painted a picture to go with the claim, STNR there beside it in a big blue swirl.

I caught Piedog's eye, we were so fucked, we were fucked on a new scale even for us, Bennie's lips moving, mouthing it like tabloid, BENNIE SUCKS COCK, as tall as a small child, sprayed on the wall, a gagging mouth beside it full of shaft and Tommy-T's Landcruiser, like a ship from heaven, purred across our vision and stopped and the dark window glass dropped and Tommy-T pointed at us and crooked his stubby finger.

Piedog would have admitted snorting the whole stash just to get out of that Ford and into the back of Tommy-T's big van and I would have admitted helping him with all the shortages too just to join him. Bennie was going to boil, the lid would come off with a 'crump' and we didn't care as long as Tommy-T got us clear and out of the Ford, Bennie like an airtight can, humming there, the pressure building, the lid about to go.

Piedog was counting out four grand. We were stashed behind the Sports Centre in Tommy's 'Cruiser, Tommy-T like a fat python wedging back between the seats.

'Where's the rest of it?' His eyes never left my face, Piedog's hand fanning fast like some slick magician, his lips moving, counting and counting.

'Down in Dessie's'. He nodded towards me and I nodded too, eager to agree.

'Yeah, and we're doing the clubs tonight. It's safe in the shed, the ould wan's never out, she's always pissed, and her lungs are fucked'.

And Piedog nodded again. 'Yeah Dessie's got it in the shed'.

Tommy kinda sighed and looked at the two of us for far too long and leaned across and scooped the fifties and tossed a few of the twenties back.

'That's good, and you'll have the balance when?' He smelled of fear, it was our fear and he was causing it.

'Weekend. By the weekend, at the latest and we'll need another batch'.

Tommy just smiled and added the folded cash to the choker he took from under the seat, pulling it out of an old black sock and told us to ring him when we had it and we piled out of the Landcruiser, then he called us back and told us to 'keep our noses clean'.

We were huddled at the back of the lockups on Pinewood, Piedog was skinning two big numbers and I suppose the cold was making his hands shake.

'Is Tommy-T wide? To us I mean?' Piedog looked at me and handed me one and we lit up and then he fished the empty wraps from his T-shirt pocket. At least we'd lost Bennie, he'd shot off in the Ford when Tommy-T beckoned, a bad feeling or some ould wound, he wouldn't say.

'How bad?' I looked at Piedog; his fringe looked frozen to his forehead, his eyes were staring, his freckles like small bullet holes around his nose, and he had yellowed punch marks around his eyes.

'Eight, that's two hundred'.

'Eight?'

'Yeah, or maybe nine, I think I might have dropped one'.

'Call it ten, that's two-fifty and how many wraps have we left?'

'Over a dozen. Ok, maybe eleven'.

'Fuck, that's a lot of starch'. And I had to laugh, the chills were hitting me and the smoke was locking me down inside and my teeth felt like chips of ice.

'Yeah, it's a lot'. Piedog squinted. He knew what Tommy-T could do, would do, even to his cousin if he found us out.

'We'll take the eleven and cut them for five extra'. I was thinking hard here.

'Yeah, or maybe cut it for four and phone Tommy-T for another batch, then we'll make up the rest from that'.

'Sledger!' And he punched my arm so hard I thought it had died. That was Piedog, either all up or all down and so our shed beckoned and we had no shortage of starch and we were off.

We could hear it coming, the crump, crump as the Focus shot the speed bumps over on the main road, squeals and the rasp of tarmac and Bennie in the Ford rounded the corner from Pinefield and locked all four to stop beside us.

'In!'

'Wha?'

'Get in! The cops are coming'. Hardly a golden invitation and we could hear the long, lonely sigh of the police siren along The Avenue but what odds? The Ford smelled of petrol and sick and the knife was still sticking from the dash and Bennie looked freaked. He'd lost his baseball cap and there were what looked like scratches on his face, little blood stitches like he'd run through briars.

He kept looking in the mirror as we sped along, the shocks bottoming on the speed bumps. He threw the car right, skipping The New Park altogether, the gates of the pitches standing open and we hit the grass sideways. We knew what was on now and Piedog began to gather the few live cans off the floor, Bennie winding the wheel.

'Out!' And he popped the bonnet sprinkling petrol from a red plastic can, opening the windows, dousing the seats, the match a flare as we stepped back, the empty can the first thing to pop and we were through the hedge before the tankful blew. Bennie was popping too, jumping straight up into the air and shouting 'Yes! Yes!' Then he stopped, all serious.

'I found Stanners, the little fuck'.

'And?'

'Swore allsorts that it wasn't him, but I doused him …'

'With petrol?'

'Yeah, lit the match and all, then the little shit ran, ran like a rat, lucky as fuck the match missed him'. And Bennie laughed, his eyes were still burning, his stare still seeing the running Stanners, the beautiful arc of the flaming match. 'Shoulda burned him ...'

Not good. I looked at Piedog, a quick nod and it might be worth mentioning Tommy-T.

'We have to 'tip' for Tommy-T, the clubs ...'

Pretended like he never heard us, he was fumbling in his pockets, came up with change and the rag end of a joint.

'I'm for the shops, I could eat ... See ya later on'. And he was gone, off down Fuchsia, his white tees flapping and his flippant, boxer walk. I looked at Piedog again.

'I wonder what it is with Tommy-T?'

'Dunno, but Tommy never says, calls him a fucking waste of space and just spits'.

But what the fuck, it got us back to the shed behind my house; we passed my mother in the kitchen in a fug of smoke, roaring at the telly, waving a can of cider like some battered flag. It took Piedog no time at all to do the balance and he slipped the pack of wraps into his trackies pocket, handed five to me.

'C'mon the bus is due. Put them away safe until I tip a dozen or so and we'll make the call to Tommy-T.

I took the five empty silver wraps and he stood at the door looking out at the dark, the ould wan was still ranting through the thin glass. I heard him ease away from the door and I pushed the father's old bicycle aside and leant well in to reach my work jeans where they hung with my shirt from the shelving. I slipped the five squares into an arse pocket rearranging the jeans to hang straight, making sure they covered the two remaining cans of powder blue spray paint, I might need them yet, and Piedog was calling that he could hear the bus.

Bennie's Case

Funny how everything happens together, all of the time. I was nearly done, we were pulled in off the slip-road down behind the pitch-and-putt course, the Singer's hairy gut, slap-slapping in my face, his hands tightening on my shaved skull, his voice tightening up to a truly rich note when I sensed the darkness and the Singer chose his big moment and shot off. I eased upright in the seat, Tommy-T's Landcruiser blocking out all the light and the Singer muttered 'fuck, fuck' and tried to tuck himself in, his shirt all sticky, his hands all wet.

'Yer a dirty little fucker, aren't ya?' Tommy-T smiled when I eased into the passenger seat; the fifty safely tucked in my T-shirt pocket. I said nothing; he'd do all the pushing here. He was eating a McDonald's meal, the chips looked tiny, like scraps in his maw grip, mauling into the cheeseburger like it was an open wound; the giant Coca-Cola abandoned in the drinks holder.

'That's dangerous work'. He was pushing again but I kept looking out the window, straightened my cap, the

Singer and his Mondeo long gone. He'd not forget the sight of Tommy-T for a long time. Fuck him anyway, he'd probably cost me a customer, and a regular one as well.

'Ya need minding. I'll do you a deal'.

'Can mind myself'.

'Hey, this is a special offer'. He pointed at the bag of food, the edges ripped, and the curry sauce running like shite. 'Think of it as a Happy Meal. Don't push it away. A hundred a week and no one will touch you. Or if you don't, no one will touch you either, that is except me and that won't be nice'. And he winked, the sweat like tears on his upper lip, a mayonnaise sheen on his stubby fingers, the smell of the curry chips making me gag. But no one went up against Tommy-T, no one. After all dead was dead. And that was it, a done deal, simple and cut.

'I'll start this week then; we'll give you freebies until Friday'.

And he balled the greasy bag and tossed it past my face through the open window and into the briars, wiping his stubby fingers on his baggy, green jumper.

'Out!'

'But ...'

'Out! Use yer fucken legs for a change; give yer gob a rest'.

I glared at him and he leant across and hooked the front of my T-shirt, pulled me towards him. The first slap took me by surprise, the full weight of his hand ringing in the second blow. He breathed heavy straight in my face, I could smell the sour tang of the burger, the laced whiff of the mayonnaise.

'Bennie, I don't like you, I never have, but this is my patch, so it all feeds through me, just like Dessie, just like Piedog. So, man, woman or small boy, I don't care what you fuck, Friday it is and we'll start then, and that'll be every Friday. OK?'

We were huddled around the big bottle of Calor gas; the four of us, like something from a bad western, taking turns. I was going easy but the others were drooling shite and trying to focus on each other and trying to push each other away. We were all huddled in the Arches, at the entrance to The Park, and there was a wind. It was the only thing blowing through because no one would come that way when the dopers stole a canister of gas and right now there was a houseful of students down in the estate with nothing cooked.

I was taking small hits just to keep them sweet and I was waiting for a car to pull up, the mobile on buzz in my trackie pocket, the fizz of it along my thigh. I wouldn't miss it that way, like I wouldn't miss the cash.

I only knew the dopers to see. I knew Tommy-T sold to them, well Dessie and Piedog did and they were his boys, but I'd never been mixed with that except to take freebees from Piedog and I'd only been sleeping in the Arches for about a week. I had Dessie's old sleeping bag stashed behind the wrecked ice-cream van, which never moved. I'd wrap myself in that and huddle in, keeping out of sight because that was the trick when you were waiting for whatever showed.

The mother had thrown me out two weeks before, saying how she couldn't stand the smell of drugs in the house any longer. I'd bunked in with Dessie for a while but I couldn't take the way his mother stretched around the house, her head in a bottle, cans everywhere, looking for matches, looking for talk, so in the end I'd taken the sleeping bag and moved. She was doing my head and it was warm, I'd have a place of my own before the weather came, maybe just a share, but I had been saving hard.

The dopers were well out of it now; the lanky guy with the pinstripe jacket over the baggy jeans was doing his version of the Vinnie dance, like his feet were set in cement, swinging his body to his own tune, his head back, and the sores around his mouth shining in the light. The other two were propped together, the big yellow bottle between them, the small guy trying to depress the nipple, hunting for another gush, his companion motionless, hunched forward his mouth already open, his eyes already fucked, gulping for gas like a stuck fish.

I felt the mobile buzz in my pocket and pushed my white cap back. Most marks liked to see your face and I eased slowly from the Arches, the Vectra already at the kerb, another regular and I lifted the door handle, a note added to the roll, money for jam.

The Vectra driver dropped me back and as I was slipping from the car he said, 'Bennie, I have friends coming in from Kildare for the weekend, they're good spenders, there's a party at the Radisson, you interested?

I nodded.

'You know them?'

'Yeah, they're sound, big money too. Billy drives a blue Merc, you can't miss it. They're into a good party. Serious lads, I'll pass on your number'.

I nodded again. I'd done parties, twos, threes and more. I'd arranged nights and done mad gigs when everything just clicked. I'd driven to Dublin once with this fat factory man and booked into a good hotel, separate bookings. The look on the face of the ponce hotel clerk, the twist in his eyes when the screen popped up and everything was prepaid, meals and bar, the lot, and he'd slipped the key-card across the marble top like he was pushing shit.

'Hey', I winked, 'don't knock it, you're sitting on a goldmine there but it's a mine, you have to drill it'. And he'd blushed puce and looked away.

I was back at Dessie's grabbing a shower and borrowing some clean togs when the mobile rang. Dessie had all his stuff spread out on the bed and we could hear his mother downstairs calling out some sad song in a dead drunken slur, something about a red dress and too much pain.

She was weeping the lyrics and Dessie kept muttering the words 'ould cunt' under his breath because he was embarrassed. I didn't want to be there either so I grabbed a set of black trackies and a white T-shirt and he called me 'a commando bollix' because I skipped the underwear, and made like to punch me on the chin and we both laughed.

Then I got out of there before his mother decided to share her marriage shit with me again, slobbering her spit down the front of my T-shirt and rubbing it in with her stubby fingers, her rings clacking as she snuffled on my shoulder, the blue light from the TV sliding off the wet sheen of the skin around her eyes. She used to be so good before she tossed Dessie's father out, now she just sucked on cans with her hair like a greasy helmet. Fuck that.

Tommy-T must have been waiting for me or maybe I was just unlucky but when he stepped out of the laneway by the shops I wasn't ready for him.

'Hey gayboy, can it be Friday already?' I backed against the wall, no sense in running. Not that the fat fucker could catch me but ... I dug into my pocket, the hundred all ready and rolled. Handed it over.

'Good boy'. He made to stroke my cheek and I pulled away so he swung instead, the punch catching me on the shoulder, deadening my arm, his grip on my throat, the weight of him pinning me against the roughness of the wall.

'Listen, ya fucker, this is an arrangement, nothing more. Business. So just be grateful. Little pricks like you are all over, so just be thankful that I'm minding you. Ok?'

He was loving this, fucken loving it and if I ever got the chance he'd love it less and less, but then there was a queue for that prize.

'How much?'

'How much what?'

'To go away? For good?'

'For good? There's no "for good" gayboy but for a "big one" I'd leave you alone, say ...' He pretended to be counting, moving his thumb across the fingers of his left hand, then on to his right. Then he scratched inside his baggy jumper, withdrew his hand and sniffed at the nails, and looked up again, pretending to think. 'Say until Christmas. I can't be fairer than that, eh Bennie?' And he slapped my cheek twice.

'A thousand?'

'Cheap at half the price, a "big one" sets you free, for now. Reckon you can get yer gob around that much cash?'

I wasn't going to tell him or fucken anything like that but I still had just over five hundred rolled in my sock and maybe, just maybe ... I made to go.

'Hey?'

'Yeah? I'll see you next Friday Tommy, see you then'.

That was it; keep the fat fucker guessing, he'd whistle until then. He was only going for it because he knew he could. He was rolling it in anyway, selling grass and coke and he had the women in Number 56, and he made lots betting on the fights, Piedog was nearly always a sure thing and that was just the stuff I knew about.

'Don't forget now'.

I raised my left hand keen to be away, the mobile buzzing in my pocket for Partytime.

We were all sitting in a circle in the big hotel, the view over the dark lake blind to us, the spinning strobe lights flashing off the glass. There were maybe eight or nine of us, the talk running in circles, the drinks easing us in, everyone on their best smile. I love that uncomfortable thing which happens sometimes with all the so-called eagles perched, their eyes hooded, their claws hooked, the blue talons just below the saggy skin and you can feel it, all the smiles like latex masks slipped over the bare burning flesh.

I was loving it, the old and the fat and the real talk, business and the law, everyone on pretend like it had already happened and this was only chat, hiding it, just hiding it, and I was the only local. I was perched between Billy and Kevin, sinking cocktails like mad, all the others sorted but you could feel the hunger, the craving need.

The Merc had been fucken huge, the purr of power from it, and the drugged smell of leather when they'd picked me up along the bus-lane. Easiest way is at a bus stop, a car looking for directions, me just waiting.

Billy and his 'friend' Kevin were old guys, maybe 50s and they looked like a couple, acted like it too. It was easy to spot the boss, the little shows, the so gentle nods, Kevin holding his replies sometimes, his eyes on Billy.

And here we were, all of us, like runners on the gun, all the delicacies to be observed, before, in twos and threes, the drifting started and Billy and Kevin sat polishing off gins until there was only us sitting in the tattered graveyard of a good night and Billy got back to talking again about some DVD he'd watched, Kevin all ears, nodding.

'Best I've ever seen. Quality'. Kevin kept nodding, his eyes flicking from Billy to me, back to Billy.

'Internet?'

'Naw, Eamonn brought it back from that last trip to Bulgaria'.

'Eamonn? Bulgaria? Hmmm'.

'Not dubbed or anything and great quality. Clear. And good action too'.

Something was pitching here; I could feel it, Billy's grim fingers stroking my thigh.

It was top quality, no flickers or bad cuts, no copy lines or sudden jumps and the actors were mostly American, big and middle-aged and doing Europe on lots of dollars a day. Most porn stars talk with their jaws set in cement, like all the energy is focussed through their cocks but these were better than most, natural, chilled. We watched them in all the usual haunts, late-night bars and dingy dives, the floorshow pumping, full of skinnies, the usual lump of sex and sweat until the big muscle guy tapped his friend and said.

'Reckon it's time for us to check in'. And then they stood and received the heavy case from the manager and walked from the bar, the staff lining up, the manager bowing, dollars dished out easy and the line of naked boys smiling, a cavalcade of pecs and perfect teeth. The Rolls slipped them into some amazing forecourt, all shooting fountains and yellow light. Next we saw them briefly on the balcony of their suite, leaning into the city blackness, the bellboy wheeling their luggage in, the one large suitcase deposited on the bedroom floor.

We were sitting on the big sofa, the three of us, the suite suitably hushed, all subdued table lamps and heavy shades, Billy and Kevin either side of me, the minibar on overtime.

'Now, here's the, the, the bit ...' Billy was stammering, his eyes burning off the screen, both of the actors stripped naked, the usual stuff until the taller of the two flicked the locks on the large suitcase and eased back the lid, a thin boy unfolding, limb on limb, rising from the dark interior, slowly, to the easeful music, his hands open, the palms turned outwards, the very centre of him opening out, unfolding upwards, the muscles of his arms lengthening, his legs lengthening and his nakedness turning like a discus thrower in the tasselled light.

Which was when the picture stilled, Billy's arm with the zapper outstretched, Kevin's lips frozen on the rim of his glass, his eyes focussing … on me?

'Now Bennie …'

I turned slowly; Billy was easing off the sofa, leaning towards the large hard-shelled suitcase upright in the corner of the room. I held his gaze. I had to know.

'How does it end?' My throat was dry and there was the metal taste of gin. I could hear Kevin lifting himself up, my eyes returning to the frozen screen.

'How does it end?'

'Oh, the usual, you've been there, you've been there. We'll pay well'. This from Billy. I looked again at the large case. He'd flicked back the polished metal lid; the interior was black and shiny.

'I'm not getting in there, no fucken way'.

'We'll pay really well'. Kevin had his wallet out, flicking fifties onto the leather sofa, my eyes following their delicate flutter, their guided flight, Billy joining him, his notes adding to the dropping flock.

'It'll just be for five minutes. While we, ah … you know, get ready, to greet you. Yes, to get ready'.

'And?'

'Then we'll let you out, naturally. Just like in the film'. He pointed to the screen again, the boy frozen there, something learned in his eyes.

'No. That's not on, no'. I felt foolish and started to turn, the DVD kicking out and the pumped-up voice of the Late News announcer filled the room, calling the last of the Euro Million numbers for the weekend, telling us the total, telling us how someone had to win.

Billy added another two fifties to the pile. I could pay Tommy-T off no bother, and probably get a room, somewhere towards the city centre, escape from the shining streets, the shit of fear, the fevered smell of gas.

'Five minutes?'

'Five. Max, while we get ready. But you have to drop the togs, you know, just like him'.

I looked again at the shuffled deck of fifties. Tommy-T could fuck himself. I scooped them into a neat deck, kicking my trainers off, slipped the money into my sock. My T-shirt came off easy, Billy's rasped breathing heavy in the room as I slipped the trackies past my knees, past my ankles, bending, stepping out of them and over the lip of the case. There was a slight draught from the open balcony door as I eased my head down into myself, my legs folding as I turned in towards the shape of the case, bending my arms, easing in until my shoulder touched the cold of the lining, Billy smiling as he lifted the shining metal lid and I closed my eyes. After all, fuck it, how dark could it get?

Blow

There were light-bursts in the drumbeats. He could see them, how he didn't know, but he could see them now. They curved from the speakers in a blue swathe, octopus smoke that cut curly-cues through the cigarette fog, sealed themselves around the bulbs, grew ghost-fingers that seemed to run through the light fittings, snaking across the ceiling, lacing through the cables, electric flashes shooting through the notes, the swirling pulses becoming sound again.

And the blue fog, iced blue coming towards him and all around him and the pounding in his ears. He'd seen Phylly turning, his dance growing more extreme, his body sheeted in sweat, turning with a sudden jerk and the pup sailing through the light, Liza, cartoon puppy with every hair on end, spiky, cartoon puppy, her fur like a scream. He could hear it in his ears as he watched her sail, her paws rigid, the fire opening up as she hit, sparks everywhere and her whimper-cry lifting him off the couch with a roar.

He was Homer now, Homer was his name, his own name was gone. He held the shotgun in his hands; it felt so soft, was it melting? He blinked to clear his eyes, blinked again, gripped it tighter, his brain trying to adjust as he moulded the triggers, his putty finger squeezing, the rush of slow-motion gold as the first barrel exploded. Had he done that? Think. He had to think. All their faces frozen, a glow around them and the snow settling on his arms. Was it snowing? A flake tickled his nose, drifting down from the hole in the ceiling. Did he do that? Looking up he thought he could see a star. How was that? Was it his?

Their voices came through the blue as he levelled the gun again.

'No Homer! No!' The barrels jerking to the beats, kicking, pounding as he tried to level them, tried to calm them, make them his. Yvonne pleading to him too, coming in from somewhere near the floor, her arms like the tentacles of a giant squid, the long nails like bloody, crimson eyes, he ducked their searching glances. He had tears in his own eyes; he wiped them with his sleeve, his bristles scraping like gunfire across the roughness. He swatted at the buzzing sound, Liza staggering from the ash-pit, shivering, and her puppy fur smouldering. Their voices were calling; he could hear the thin girls.

'Homer! No!'

'Let me think!' He roared. 'Fuckers! Let me think!'

That morning he thought he'd seen a tumbleweed in the rain. He pulled in a doorway as it cart-wheeled up past the Polish shop, the squall whipping it. He rested his hand on an imaginary pistol butt, a Johnny Cash tune bleeding in his head. He watched it as it spun past Quigley's Hypermarket, stuck for a moment behind a refuse bin before kicking high into the empty coal-bag it really was, the rain peppering it and he shook his head, pulled hard on the hood of the anorak like a Stetson brim; hung-over mornings could be like that.

The pup wrestled in his breast, squeezing her brown head through the zippered top of his heavy anorak. It was snug in there in the rug of the coat. He knew its warmth, stiffened as it was by nature and calling, stiffened as it was by salt stains and fish scales and Guinness and spatterings of gut-bile, stiffened as it was by body fluids, mostly his own and blessed for it, the hood like a cave mouth round his shaggy curls. He stroked the pup's furry crown with his thumb, felt the thin haunches shiver in the cup of his other hand as he crooned to the flickering ears. Tinker's pup maybe and a hard night behind her down at the travellers' site but he would sell her on, even if she was the travellers' gift, or maybe he wouldn't bother, time would let him know.

He faced towards Quinn's Bar, no sign of Tommy-T yet, the tumbleweed coal-bag wrapped around the electric pole outside the new apartments with the fake Irish name, Garraí Eamonn.

The mornings were often like this since the fucking skinhead died, not that it was Bartley's fault but the pub owners weren't having it and he was gone, job gone, house gone, marriage gone, home gone but he could doss at the back of Kirby's, not much more than a shed but it was dry. Yes, it was dry.

A hard night all right, his head was lifting. Where the fuck did the travellers get the Guinness, kept going to the back of the Land Cruiser and coming back with pints of draught, there was even grass floating in one of them, tasted fine though, but draught, on a halting site? Fuck sake and the kids lippin' it too and smoking as well. There weren't even wheels on the 'Cruiser, dead for years by the look of it. And he'd sat by the fire, Tommy-T keeping him in chat about the next deal and giving the odd clip to the kids, didn't matter whose kids they were. Reminded Bartley of how it used to be, everyone responsible, not like now, but Tommy-T still had it and the women too, yeah, and that Big Mary wore them tight. God his eyes hurt.

He squinted towards the block of new apartments: Garraí Eamonn, where had they got the name? The Irish names were important now, a selling point with their pristine gardens, Garraí Eamonn with its twelve parking spaces for its eight apartments, all apart, the occupants apart, their breaths held living there, where no-one cried for the morning, where no-one missed the tangle-tongued togetherness of his own childhood.

That was all gone and he cried for it, not tears but inside where his heart was, in there he cried. Imagine living that close to others and knowing no-one. Garraí Eamonn, imagine coming up with a shite name like that? He could remember when the council houses were there, a little backwater, everyone living on nothing and now that was all bulldozed and the apartment block had sprung up and no one knew who the owner was but judging by the cars the occupants weren't on the dole, no, not on the dole; no 'government artists', that's for sure.

He was on a slow pint in the afternoon when they bustled in and the skinny woman went straight for the pup lapping Guinness from the burger box where Bartley had fed her chips after he'd had the Supermacs meal earlier.

Must be the crowd up at Crowley's. These were the English musicians that all the talk was about, the whole house taken, stables and all and Martin had told him about the sounds he'd heard, even above the engine of the van when he'd delivered the extra bags of groceries. Not like music, no, more like beating a heavy drum, boom, boom, thump, thump, and wires everywhere. But he'd bought Bartley a pint from the twenty euro tip they'd given him and that was fine.

The skinny woman led him through the open door with its sheen of red paint and the big brass knocker with the sunray face reminding him. He'd last been here with his father when he was a kid, must be forty years at least; they'd put the turf around the back. The Americans liked the smell of it when they stayed, the 'authenticity' as George Crowley had called it. He hadn't heard that word in Quinns ever, not a word that got a lot of use and now the house looked different. Black cables ran along the dull mosaics, the floors a tangle through the double doors as she led him in, the small pup squirming in his breast and the sound of the running music ... how would he put it? Rhythm but not like country, the sound thumping and two men with film cameras feeding from a box of wires.

Jesus, maybe this was a mistake. Did he need the work? A patrol she'd said, Yvonne, her thin body hip-hugging the bar, her first pint before him.

'Jamie needs patrols darling, security, we spoke this morning. They've begun already, the groupies, and he's only here a week. Phylly gets in later today and that'll really bring them on'.

'Patrols?'

'Someone to keep the watchers away from the house, the young girls, mostly at the weekends. Jamie needs this new CD. He needs to keep the push on, burn it fast, and hold the sales? George Crowley said there was a gun thingy?

So here he was, Bartley, nearly sixty, in his stiff, dull-sheen anorak following this thin woman, who must be almost as old as himself, who called him 'darling' and introduced him as 'security' to all the others. The house was full of people in crazy looking clothes and full with the thump of music the cry of mean guitars. He knew Johnny Cash would have hated it.

'Bart you say?'

'Bartley'.

The kid stood before him in a pair of tracksuit bottoms and a v-neck woolly sweater, a set of headphones around his neck.

'Bartley? Like in Bartley Simpson?' And everybody laughed. If this was down in Quinns he'd lose teeth for that and slide on his arse towards the narrow door too.

'We'll call you Homer then. OK? Now Homer, what I need is ... security, someone to keep the kids away from the windows and off the grounds'.

'Kids?'

Jamie stared at the floor. His eyes looked sorta crazy, Bartley thought, staring and kinda starry.

'Yeah teenies mostly. We get lots of girls, kids, trying to get in and meet Phylly and me. It's very flattering and we do pick and choose. But now we're working so... no play today'. And he looked directly at Bartley.

'There's a shotgun in the stables. George said we could use it, he doesn't shoot anymore. Don't shoot anyone Homer but ... look the part. Two hundred a day? You can shoot?'

'Yes'. Two hundred a day. And Bartley remembered the rusty single-barrel, his father out for rabbits, the pot ready, the big to-do, the rows at home after his sister said they looked like skinned babies.

'Here we go Jamie!' One of the lads at the table called, stabbing buttons on a flat panel and the room filled with drums. Jamie turned his stare to the floor and stood motionless except for the rapid flick of his left hand, following the beat as it built, the rhythm growing faster, twisting in on itself, gaining speed until it almost became a whistle, the beat racing ahead trying to catch itself and almost succeeding.

And the deeper rhythms fed in, locked with the main one, raced around it, worrying it like an angry wasp, goading it. Jamie began to tremble, his legs joining the race, his head snapping, moving towards the speakers, spreading his arms wide above his head, a heavy pressure building and building, Jamie racing with it now until, without warning it stopped dead, the room frozen in its own silence.

'That's it so far Jamie, not bad?' And Jamie nodded, seemed lost for a moment before he turned and took Bartley's arm leading him from the room.

'You like drum n' base?'

'Ah, they don't play it much at Quinns, it's more of a country music pub, Johnny Cash, ya know?'

And Jamie had nodded again, but said nothing.

The stables were lower than he remembered them, the roof planks almost touching his hood, the she-pup walking shaky-like on the shiny, uneven cobbles. They were in the narrow space behind the tack-room, Jamie and himself and Yvonne never far away as Jamie pointed to the single bed.

'Kip down in here if you like Homer, walk the gardens and carry the gun with you, just for show mind, ok?' He pointed to the polished double-barrel lying broken open on the table, the box of shells.

'It'll be quiet in the mornings, always is, no-one shows until the afternoon, but you could be out until five?' The question in his voice.

'Five? In the morning?'

'Yeah, the fans can be a tricky lot … a tricky lot'. And he'd laughed that funny, high pitched giggle again, his eyes and the spiky hair adding to Bartley's impression of some new type of species he'd never met before. Never.

'There's always food in the kitchen'. Yvonne eased in from the side again. 'Jamie has a chef in and the larder's full of beer'.

And so he'd swung out that evening, the remains of a beef sandwich in his hand made with some strange type of bread, another in his gut and the double-barrel on his arm, two extra shells in his pocket, the gun broken open just to be safe. He did a quick sweep along the boundary fences, looking for gaps, drank the salt taste of the evening, chewed to the crunch of the sea-grass on his boots, his belly full of good beef and the three Heinekens swinging in his coat.

He brought Liza along inside his anorak. They'd named her Liza gathered around the big table in the library, the surface covered in paper and discs and small machines he didn't understand, the 'crew' as Jamie called them all gathered around, the beats filling the big room.

'You're Homer mate, so she's gotta be Liza, yeah Liza with a Zee, ok? Innit?' The little waif who played the keyboards had offered as she stroked the pup's cold nose, the pup wagging her little blunt stump of a tail and licking her hand.

'Zee? Oh Zed, we call it Z'. And Bartley had smiled. So Liza it was for now anyway and he stood on the headland and looked across the shore towards Ardfry and the Creganna uplands and cracked another tin feeling the cold beer-tongue slide down his throat, cutting through the phlegm of last night's Guinness. He could see the traveller site, down towards the army barracks, the flag still flying and the steady clatter of machinegun fire, showed it to Liza, tickled her jowls and whispered 'home' in her furry ear, hawked and spat. Yep, things could be a lot worse.

When they came the first time they drove straight up the avenue, sweeping through the trees in a battered Fiat Panda. He just got a glimpse from the hill of the skinny girl easing the gates open, her thin back bent, long hoodie and tight jeans before she jumped back into the passenger seat and the little car moved forward.

'Fuck them! The bitches!' And he threw the dregs of another Heineken can in the ditch and started to run. Fuck them, the hill uneven under his boots as he descended with the shotgun in one hand and Liza whimpering in the other. They'd got past him, no two ways about it. He shambled past the bay windows; the car parked there, the doors open, the hall door open too, the music pumping. Fuck them.

'Homer!' Jamie sat smothered in cushions and girls on the big couch, all the others lying around. The cans were out, bottles of spirits too.

'Homer!'

He felt big and out of breath. The gun felt big, Liza had pissed on his arm, he could feel the warm trickle. Jamie was off the couch, the girls falling together. Bartley knew his mouth was open.

'Homer, this is Phylly'. And the tallest, thinnest black man Bartley had ever seen padded behind him carrying a gigantic sandwich on a plate.

'Hello Homer'. American, his hand out Bartley struggling with the gun, trying to squeeze it and Liza into one paw, the piss dripping off his sleeve.

'Ah, maybe not now Homer my man, maybe another time'. He'd taken the huge sandwich instead, his mouth snaking around the edges, dripping juices, the girls giggling.

'Sorry Mr ... Jamie'. Bartley pointed towards the girls, now there were only two. He'd spotted three?

'It's ok Homer, old friends. I had to welcome Phylly properly; they'll be gone again tomorrow'. And he dived back into the cushions the girls climbing on his back burying him in the softness.

Starry night, Bartley sat in the purple glow, his back to a tree, he could see the orange burn of the town, a satellite crawled across the heavens, and do they see me he wondered as he tilted another can.

He'd hunted a gang of locals around eleven, full of beer and smelling for a party, the sight of the shotgun had been enough. Joey Connor's son was one of them, trying to be a DJ in the new pub near Garraí Eamonn, Bartley had seen the posters, 'DJ DafBus meets The Bee Bop Baluba, Live from the Congo!' it said, or some shite like that, Connors little pimpled face orange in the glow beside a smiling black man.

Smart little fucker though and two of the Quinlans with him, the twins, two little bitches. Would they be seventeen? Hardly. They'd fucked him out of it but he'd held firm even told the Connor's lad to stick to the fishing as he'd closed the gates.

'Fuck off, ya wanker!' The thinner of the twins had called as she'd climbed back into Connor's van, two other cars speeding away, her skimpy dress hiding very little. 'Ya tosser!'

He took a swing behind the stables sometime after two, climbing the slope, a sliver of gutted moon hung above the forestry behind the house, the wind sighing through the tops with a displeased whisper. The house was a lighted ship below him, all the windows glowing bright, the door standing open. He could see people on the upper floors, bodies running, the thin girls moving in his imagination, their clipped actions, and their sudden darts.

Behind the house something slipped towards the stables; a doorful of light escaped over the cobbles; someone had gone into the tack room. He dropped down the narrow path, the rose brambles pulling at his sleeve as he jogged. He could see nothing through the window, the big room empty except for the saddles astride the wooden rails, the winkers hanging on the iron hooks.

If the young lad of the Connor's or the two Quinlans had come back he'd give them 'tosser', he fucken would. He eased open the door to his room, Phylly sat at the small table his eyes bloodshot in the shaving mirror, but fixing on the barrels of the shotgun.

'Homer!' And he leant forward, a great sniffing inhalation filling the small space, then another and he blinked, his eyes tearing, wiping flecks of white from his nostrils.

'Wha? ... ah, Phylly?' Bartley knew that people took drugs, had often seen them but it was their business, he'd tried the weed and the odd pill but nothing more, he'd seen it in the pubs, but Guinness was his poison. He looked at the plastic bag.

'Homer, my man, Jamie doesn't really like it when I use when we're working and yes this is cocaine hydrochloride. Cocaine. Up the nose and no-one knows, as they say. Cocaine? Snow? Blow?' Phylly laughed and turned and separated a small amount from the mouth of the open bag, chopping it with a black card, lining it up in two thin chalk dust lines.

'Here we go'. He pointed to Bartley. 'Give it a shot, my man, it's harmless Homer, here we go'. He bent again and sucked a sharp intake, first one nostril then the other, then the tears, quick flick, lick of the tongue, dabbing the flecks from the table and rubbing his gums.

Bartley approached the table and leant in, he'd tried most everything, so what odds? Phylly separated a thin line and offered it, pushed the short tube into Bartley's hand and Bartley inhaled, the punch as each snort hit behind his eyes.

Phylly was steady. He placed a hand on Bartley's shoulder, gripped it tight.

'Gold, pure gold, it gives you the edge, makes you hot!' And he laughed, easing his lanky frame through the door. 'So hey! We need the heat to feel the beat'.

And Bartley watched him cross the courtyard, Phylly with his fingers clicking, his head bobbing, forward, back, forward, back. Fuck it, he cracked another tin, the heat of the hit behind his eyes, this was getting very strange and he sank a half, tipped a trickle into Liza's bowl, setting her down on her shaky pins, 'pissed puppy' she'd called her, the pup settling on her heels before staggering to bury her nose in the frothy amber. 'Pissed puppy', he laughed, feeling a little light, a shot of blue, repeating Yvonne's comment earlier from the pub.

It was much later, he'd lost count now but he imagined he was drunk. There was no-one. He thought he'd heard a car but the avenue was clear, the headland seemed steeper, he stopped to catch his breath. He could hear the wind in the tops, the sky parting like a golden eyelid. Must be well after five now, he thought, the sun sending a lighthouse beam across the shore. The mudflats were blue daubs, with waders feeding at the edges. He was watching the tide, the drug-hum filling him, capturing the sea as it came claiming everything, running along the shallows, filling the shore like a jigsaw, etching out each stone, each pebble, filleting mud shapes from the flats, licking runnels through the sand until the whole shore was a sheen of sunlight and the bay was full and he unzipped himself and pissed on the thistles, threw the last empty can in the ditch and turned towards the house.

Yvonne was smoking a cigarette at the open door, her arms hugging herself; it was very cold.

'Homer', she cried. 'Just in time for the party, well, the end of the party'. She giggled, her voice sounded brittle, like a delicate glass ornament shattering.

'Come in, come in'. And she staggered slightly as she turned and slipped her arm in his.

The table held the litter of a good time, bodies everywhere, the music loud and the lights spinning. Someone pushed a tumbler of spirits in his hand and he drank. Liza gave a groan from inside his coat as he settled in the big armchair, the fire warming him. He rested the gun, tried to take in the talk, he tried to follow the music too but it was too much, so he drank.

Yvonne settled on the arm of the chair and put her arm on his shoulder, time seemed to hang, seemed to shimmer from the ceiling, the flames licking at his eyelids, he drifted with them.

They were kissing, Yvonne holding his face, pulling him towards her, her tongue darting, then she broke away from him and he saw the dancers, they hadn't been there before. The floor was a snake pit of people, Phylly stood out like a black pole, he was wearing only tracksuit bottoms his body shining as he snaked, rivulets of sweat running over his skin. He was unflagging, hugging a girl here, backing on to Jamie as they shoulder-danced, dropping down almost to the floor before he broke away, waving the plastic powder bag, inhaling a large pinch from the back of his hand, his eyes rolling with the snort.

Yvonne appeared again and dragged him to the floor and he was shuffling with them in his heavy boots, his anorak around him like a blanket, Liza in his hand, her puppy eyes closing, giving little groans. Phylly was chanting some mad cry and Yvonne took the bag from his outstretched hand and pressed a rough pinch to her own nostrils then to Bartley's and he sniffed. Another snort and she kissed him again, her tongue in his mouth as she clung to him. She felt too soft to touch so he squeezed, her yelp lifting him as she locked her legs around his waist, a flush gaining in his head, tiny buzz lights bursting, Liza held aloft like a golden orb as the American reached and took the puppy.

Phylly's ribcage shone with streams of black sweat, his song a high-pitched yelping bark as he screamed something across the floor to Jamie, then he screamed again 'doggystyle' and tossed the puppy. Jamie crying raucous cheers catching Liza while Yvonne helped Bartley to another snort and the tears were blue again, there were pin-holes through his lighting eyes and a burning rush; he was a giant now, wrapped in a blue more blue than heaven, the tears running through his stubble. He could feel the tears as they touched each individual bristle, like the sea's edge through shore grass. There were bands of blue shooting from the speakers, his blue heart pulsing with the beats and he staggered back to the chair, Yvonne clinging to his back.

'Hello Bartley'.

The Quinlan twins were pinning young Connors to the couch, all their clothes were gone, they shone of light, their skins an amber gold, Connors nakedness a hairless, putty white.

'How?' Bartley groaned but Yvonne smothered him, shushed him, her forehead pressed to his.

'We're all so welcome here'. She slurred, this blue woman, and he pulled her closer, tried to kiss her again, but missed. Phylly faced the speakers, the blueness breathing through him, his back a ripple as he turned, his dance becoming more extreme, his body sheeted in sweat, turning with a sudden jerk as he shot and the puppy was sailing through the light, cartoon puppy with every hair on end, spiky, her fur like a scream as she sailed …

He could hear his own voice pleading, crying for more time. The shotgun became his arm, the Quinlan twins struggling with their jeans as his arm swung, young Connors cowering behind them, the barrels curving like some massive steel erection, the room growing still before him, everyone locked in place. He could hear Yvonne's voice pleading from somewhere down between his legs, Phylly's eyes fixed on the jerking barrels, Jamie's plea of 'steady mate', Liza staggering against his boot, sneezing, and her fur a smoky cloud. He could hear their pleas begging him to put it down, the blue shooting towards him once more and all around him. He gripped the stock tighter. He'd smelled burning fur before, remembered it from long ago, how much it hurt.

'No! Let me fucken think!' He roared again.

Give Them Nothing

Give them nothing. Even now he'd give them nothing. Tommy can smell the petrol and hear its slow almost chatty trickle, so there's a pipe fractured somewhere underneath and the Land Cruiser is tilted up at a mad angle and from here he can see the metal grille of the Mercedes van like old style prison bars with the flickering headlight slatting through it.

He's trying to laugh at the good of it but it makes the bullet holes bubble so he won't be doing that too often. He wants to laugh too because he thought it would hurt more, the young lad jumping from the van even before they'd stopped sliding, the Land Cruiser and the heavy van locked together. Tommy had screamed at the shock of it, screamed again at the way the lad had held the gun, almost like a ray-gun from some mad film and how he'd turned it sideways delicately, like he was offering Tommy a handshake and pumped two fast ones into Tommy's chest. How he'd cried: 'Hey there Tommy-T', as he did it and Tommy had felt the knockback of the hits, the hard blows throwing him up against the seat and then forward again. The kid had panicked then and the third shot had cut a skin flap from the top of Tommy's head, hair and scalp and blood everywhere but not the coup-de-grace the kid had thought and it left Tommy keeled over, his right leg mangled between the twisted mess of the brake and clutch pedals.

He knows that everything is only a matter of time, just like always but so much clearer now, more definite and he can hear the wheeze and rattle of the mechanics, the fuel pump still ticking even after the crash, the Mercedes leaping out from the side road to ram the Land Cruiser against the tree trunks, the sigh and moan of it, the big diesel engine straining, all the metal spinning and then the hissing calm as both engines die.

Then the driver was shouting 'Go! Go!' the gunman's trackies flashing, his trainers rasping on the gravel and the hand stabbed through the open window, the delicate twist and the exploding punches, his calm greeting, the getaway car already rolling, Tommy's vision blurred as they jumped in and sped away, uphill at a crazy angle, just a pair of kids, a gunman and a driver, almost nothing really.

Now Tommy can hear the shuffle of footsteps out there somewhere in the dark, the vertical lines of the tree trunks peeling white in the fading headlights, the branches like skinny arms, skinny fingers twitching and no matter how he turns his head the watcher is remaining out of sight, for now at least. So all he can do is wait and give it a turn and fear the trickle of fuel, the trickle of blood and the asthmatic wheeze of the ticking pump.

He has to smile though when he remembers how they'd joked, Eileen and himself, when he was leaving the caravan earlier in the evening and she pointed to his shoes, the leather cracked and a mouth appearing along the outside edge.

'Them shoes are on their last legs'. She said standing in the doorway of the caravan and the more he thought about it the funnier it got. He promised to call into the shopping centre and pick up a new pair but the cash collection down by Blake's wood came first and now here he was and her words were getting funnier than ever.

He'd gone on his knees that day up in the hospital when they'd rushed Eileen in. That was years ago now but he could still remember the saggy stretcher and how they'd slipped her into the ambulance, the sirens bouncing as they hit the tarmac out of the halting site and Tommy had tried to keep up in the old Transit, the load of scrap he'd bought earlier in the day like a fucking airbrake holding the old van back.

He'd gone on his knees in the yellowish, sticky light, the curtain drawn around her bed, the bandage like a swollen turban wrapping her shaven head and he'd promised Jesus and her that if she pulled through she'd never need again, never need anything if she survived and stayed with him. There would be no more children either, happy with the three they had and he'd be a better husband and mind her through everything too.

He had been as good as his word, the growth benign and the consultant telling him how 'they'd got it all', and that Eileen had a long battle ahead of her but that she would be fine, hedging around whether she'd ever taken any blows to the head or anything like that and backing off when he felt the cold coming off Tommy because he'd never hit his wife or any woman, never, ever.

Sure, he'd hit people for years, settled things with his fists. Once he'd fought Johnny Gauley for the best part of an hour up the Crescent, battering each other up and down two roads, the referees keeping them going, keeping it fair until Tommy had broken him outside his own door. Gauley's own family screamed at him to stand up and fight and Tommy had finished him with a sledgehammer left, tipping him over the garden wall of the house where he'd settled and Tommy's own men had helped him into the back of his van and he'd slept for two days, too sore to move, but he'd never hit Eileen, never, ever.

His 'friend' is moving again, Tommy tried turning a little but the front of his jersey was a sticky mess and he felt tired. He can hear the shuffling of his trainers like the ghost is looking him over. He tried raising his bulk but the metal held him and the pain in his chest burned like hell when he moved. Then the whiff of the cigarette wafts in and he'd have died for one drag of that sweet weed, but his throat closed on the word and he can hear the drip, drip of the petrol, the fractured pipe, so maybe not.

It had changed him though, Eileen getting sick like that. It changed how he worked. He already knew the vans that carried drugs even though nothing was said and he'd been asked himself to bring the packages across from the docks.

But the next time they'd asked he'd agreed and it had grown from there. He left the scrap behind and took on his own run. He got in early and started small, dealing weed and a few prescription pills when he could get them and when the 'E' started and powder became the game he was already there, a big man by then and feared. He never touched any of that himself but it made him hard and now all he had to do was sit in the Land Cruiser and drive, trail his slaves and take the cash.

So he trailed his lads around, telling them where to be, where to pick up and stash, where to drop off and never, ever carrying anything himself but the roll of notes under the seat, with more stuffed behind Eileen's dresser in the new 'van'. They'd even built in a hidey-hole, the carpenters, when he'd ordered the caravan for her and paid in cash too.

When Eileen's sister had married one of the Shanleys he'd had a hell of a time getting a hotel to take the wedding and he'd still be looking if he hadn't clicked the manager of The Arms was one of his buying clients, told him as much in his office, his nose wrinkling at Tommy's smoky tang.

'We need a hotel for a wedding and you know me and I know you. You won't fuck me around, willya?' That was all he had to say and the manager's eyes wavered and he'd agreed. Tommy didn't have to sledge him or anything, eased him in by promising that there would be no trouble and there hadn't been, even when they'd slung the regular bar staff out and took over the pulling themselves and Tommy had told the head barman to count the barrels and the bottles and stick to the tills, still struggling to keep up with the ching, ching as they drank the hotel dry.

And when two of the younger lads, full of Harp or Smithwicks started to square up, Tommy had hopped them together hard and left them to sleep it off in the car park, took the opportunity to haul the two black sacks full of notes from the jeep and into the manager's office and asked him for the bill. He enjoyed it a little when the manager and his assistant had gone on their knees to count out the thousands, smoothing out the crumpled fifties, covering the wedding bill in full. Tommy told him how he wasn't the best at the counting himself. He'd even slipped a couple of wraps in with the tip he eased into the manager's hand when they'd shook on a good day's work and the manager had told him 'anytime, anytime'.

But Tommy would give them nothing outside; you earn the wrong name for yourself doing that. People respect hard so he gave them hard, and it didn't matter women or men, boys or the small child. Take Number 56, he'd fallen into it almost by accident but now he had a team of good foreign girls in there working their backs off, a new crew swinging in every month or six weeks or so all arranged, lots of men now with the 'lovesick blues' and he gave good value. He had Spotter handling it for him, all his wages up his nose but streetwise, just a business arrangement but Tommy handled the security, leant in when it was needed, dipped in as well now that Eileen was so frail, but that was all just business and sex was sex.

Sometimes in the dark he'd sit on the hill above the church and watch the clients come and go, some of them double-jobbers, buying coke or pills in the clubs in town and coming to the house as well, on his payroll for drugs as well as women but that bought them no leeway. Tommy's boys parked their middle-class cars in the church grounds, always well away, and brought them back when their minute was up.

Tommy can hear him shuffling again like he's out there measuring something and the time is fuzzy anyway. It could be a minute or an hour since the whole thing kicked off and he knows he's drifting in and out, beginning to feel the cold of the night, the chill in his legs and it's getting foggy too. Tommy would try calling out but the 'ghost' is the only one out there and he's already made some decision just by sitting there out of sight and smoking, like the jury's out but the decision is already in, so there's no use calling out anything.

There were always fights. For as long as Tommy can recall, even as children they had to fight, the schoolyard like a battlefield where you fought for your family and it hardened him and he could remember his first money fight. He was seventeen and they'd driven for over an hour, no mobiles to call each other in, all arranged beforehand, word of mouth but no-one thought of backing out and they came together on a bog road off a midlands back road outside Banaher and he'd hammered one of the

Tracey's who'd been killed on a motorway outside Birmingham afterwards.

Not like now with video cameras, DVDs and mobile phones, everything a big event, young fellows getting it all for the record and Tommy could clear thousands on one fight. Piedog was a good example, cousin or not, he'd done well, still only twenty-three and razor sharp, cutting them and cutting them, Tommy's best fighter by far, even if his friends were little fuckers, but nowhere near as good as Eamonn, his big brother, but that was another story altogether.

Tommy had seen his mother once, it was when Eileen was touch-and-go and he'd driven up the country to his own family grave to say a prayer. While he was standing there in the late afternoon, the graveyard empty except for himself, the sun in his eyes, the metal grind of a train stopping in the distance, he'd seen her by the ornate carved headstone smiling at him and younger than when she'd died. He was calmer then, his eyes almost closed as he'd looked to the skies and begged, his mother nodding and smiling to him and he'd driven home, Eileen coming back to herself quickly after that.

Eamonn had been a class apart, the best fighter Tommy had ever seen, probably good enough to make any team but he'd loved to punch it out. It wasn't about name of fame or anything like that, it was personal with him, the push to be better than anyone, the need to go up against someone, any opponent and it didn't matter whether they were bigger or stronger, younger or older or faster and he'd brought big purses to Tommy when he needed them. He took the best in the country, all-comers, big and bigger, his fists weaving sorcery, clipping them until they called enough, cutting them down. But he'd gotten greedy, putting into Tommy for bigger and bigger shares and Tommy knew he was earning it, but when the word got back he was thinking of starting to deal for himself, splitting Tommy's territory, then it was time.

He can hear the footsteps moving again, he was scouting behind the Land Cruiser now, checking things out, and he felt the metal body tilt as he leant into the rear windows, one of Tommy's own then, and he had to wonder who. He was 'whizzing the van' to see what was on offer, the leeching scent of the cigarette tantalisingly close, Tommy inhaling the second-hand smoke like it was life itself.

It had taken him a month but he'd contacted Mister Hall. Everyone called him that, like London feared him and Tommy had ferried across. He'd told Tommy when they'd first met how he fucking hated 'Pikey Paddies' and Tommy had said he felt the same about 'fucking Black n' Tan Brits' but they'd always dealt well and when Tommy had asked him for a ringer Mister Hall had smiled and searched and came up with Warness, ex-British army. He'd cut Eamonn down to size.

Except no-one had told Eamonn and he kept climbing off Spotter's knee, climbing and climbing, coming up for more, Tommy even pleading with him towards the end to stay down, that he'd had enough. He'd never wanted Eamonn dead just trimmed down to size, manageable, like everyone, but Eamonn didn't get it and that day it killed him.

It would never come back to Tommy unless Mister Hall talked and hell would freeze two foot thick before that happened. They'd left Eamonn's body at the hospital doors for the doctors to find and no-one spoke and a year or so later Piedog had taken his place.

The face when he saw it was a surprise to Tommy, the razor-cut and the slicked fringe, Piedog sniffing like a wary house pet easing his head through the open window, flinching when he saw Tommy's mangled leg, the steering column pushed sideways, the pedals all awry like a bear-trap holding him. Tommy tried to talk but it came out as a ragged whistle, another gout of blood soaking through the woven mess.

'Easy now'. Piedog leant across and touched his shoulder, smoothing the tangled belt, stretching down feeling for the release between the seats but not reaching it. He tried the door but the impact had wedged it shut the Mercedes van almost resting on the bonnet of the Cruiser, waves of heat still rising from the mangled innards.

'Easy now'. He whispered again his hand stretching down until he found what he was looking for, the bloody sock slipping from under the seat and Tommy groaned, his eyes widening, a gargle of his own blood rising in his throat. Piedog considered the swollen bundle, the half-smoked cigarette coming to his lips.

'I'll mind this for you before the ambulance comes'. That was all he said, taking a quick drag and Tommy relaxed a little, he would be alright after all. He'd minded Piedog well, even put up with his friends, he was a good lad, fast with his hands, and Tommy had always treated him fair, paid him well and never gypped him when he cut the powder a little tight. Yes he'd known, but blood was blood. Tommy spat a mouthful, fixed his eyes on the smouldering butt and nodded. Piedog considered the glowing tip, sniffed once at the petrol smell, still hefting the sock.

'Are you sure?'

Tommy nodded, he could taste that drag, would clinch it between his lips until the ambulance arrived, the petrol pooling on the ground but still far enough away from him and blood didn't burn. Piedog reddened it, leant in again and placed the butt carefully between Tommy's crusted lips and Tommy inhaled, the smoke making his eyelids flutter, a racking cough shaking his frame.

Tommy nodded at Piedog as he stepped back, easing the bloody roll into his hoodie pocket, patting the shiny material flat. He lifted his trainers high as he stepped from the pooled leakage, wiped them on the stiff grass and flipped his phone, a ghostly blue lighting up his face. Then he paused and reached into the hoodie pocket again and produced the packet of cigarettes, shook it and brought it to his mouth, pinching one between his lips. The flare of the match seemed to make his eyes glint and glitter as he touched the sulphured flame to the tip, turned to face Tommy fully, the cigarette twitching.

'I'll tell Eamonn you're coming'. He pressed the phone to his ear, the blue halo around his head, the flaming match arching towards the pooled petrol and Tommy heard his own scream die in the crump as the petrol ignited and hell burned deep inside it.

Pump

You could never tell with Gary, that pinched-in, blank-faced look, the polished front of it. He'd said the shotgun was buried in the woods when they were tooling along in the stolen Vectra. Then when they'd stopped at a rusted farm gate down a side road beyond Ashbourne, the trees a waving green wall in the light breeze he'd searched out a particular tree and begun to shin up the broad trunk.

He seemed to be going high as well. Stevie could hear his grunts as he disappeared upwards, the odd muttered 'fuck' drifting down as he climbed, a skinny, denimed squirrel, hopping, moving upwards in a grunting zigzag branch-dance.

Then there was the snap high up, more swearing followed by a falling, rustling swish and a black, mould-stained package hit one of the lower branches, spun once and thudded in the dry leaves at Stevie's feet. He could hear Gary fucking like wildfire, the swearing continuing as he dropped quickly down from the leafy heights.

'Don't touch it! Don't touch it! I'm coming'. And he swung down from the lowest branch, wiping green stains from his denim jacket.

'Here', he took the heavy package and pushed it at Stevie. 'You open it'.

Stevie stripped away the heavy tape, the refuse sack ripping in places as he pulled until he tore an opening and pulled the sawn-off shotgun from the plastic shroud.

He'd seen sawn-offs in the past few years, double barrels mostly but this one was a beauty. The single barrel had been cut away almost level with the wooden grip; the stock was gone too except for a sanded, wooden knob, smoothed so smooth that it seemed to whisper for a palm to cup it.

'Don't ask me nuthin', was all Gary said when Stevie eased his finger along the barrel and cupped the cutaway stock, swinging the pump in a broad arc, his eyes on Gary's face and Stevie had left it at that. What he didn't know couldn't kick his door in at four am and nail him to the bed with lead rivets. That was how he saw it.

He pressed his face close, sniffed the dark metal. The feed slot for the shells was polished and well-used and the whole thing reeked of oil. It had seen service and he wondered where, but it really didn't matter, Gary had it now and they were on their way west to sort out a problem for one of the boss's best buyers. So the boss said and the boss knew everything.

Felicity had started again that morning when he told her he had to go. 'We could go to Liverpool Stevie; my sister said that Bren would set us up'. She was looking right at him, the baby trying to swallow her own little hand while Felicity tried to burp her.

'Fucking scousers, no way!' He'd slammed his hand down hard on the shiny worktop.

'Can Bren give us all this?' He swept his hand to take in the flat, the widescreen, the sound system, all the other good stuff.

'Can he give us what we have here? Well, can he?' The rent clear for six months, all paid, and cash in their pockets.

'Well, can he Flick? No. A job on the buildings, hiking shite up seven floors, renovating flats. No way Flick, I'm not doing that again, no way'.

'But things are coming too close here. I just can't take it anymore Stevie'. He could see the tears in her eyes and he knew she was right. Brando's boys emptied a clip into their last place, glass everywhere and Stevie lying across her, the bump between them. Then they heard the sirens rolling in from the main road and the police torches lit up the holes in their first floor windows, the ceiling so much shredded plaster.

They'd moved flats, Millie had been born and now almost a year had passed and there was more talk of Brando pushing for their heads, with Tyrell and the big boys driving around in armoured Beamers brought in from Germany while Gary and Stevie had to do with boosting a fucking Vectra off the street and be happy with it too.

They were locked into it now, their own private civil war. Drugs war for territory and it was getting more American by the day with Tyrell gone all corn rolls and black suits, expecting them all to call him Ty-rell, like the American way, even though he was from Ringsend, chalk white with it and it was just getting madder and madder.

He watched the way Gary's hands held the wheel. Funny how he could load on the 'blow' and be out of his head for days at a time and still work through it and it was difficult to tell if he was buzzing or not.

Gary was Tyrell's main shooter, a little runt of a guy with dark, almost woven hair, his cheeks always in need of a shave and eyes that could burn you down. Stevie had known him since school, could handle him after a fashion and was usually the wheelman when Gary did a job. Gary liked to drive too, it kept him calm so Stevie was happy to be the passenger sometimes and, after all, Gary had the pump.

They'd had a couple of steadiers off the kitchen worktop before they left Stevie's flat, Gary feeling the air.

'What's up with her?' he asked as they sat into the Vectra. 'Is she miserable or what?' He pronounced all four syllables of the word miserable and Stevie had mumbled about how her sister was on her case and they left it at that.

Now they were well beyond Athlone, the motorway like a magic carpet whisking them and Gary was on the phone to this pikey arranging the meet. They'd really fought before Gary arrived, Flick threatening that 'she'd be well gone' by the time he'd get back. She'd gone to her mother's before but he'd get her back, he always did even though she'd screamed and said that this time it was different.

'We're meeting him on the way in', Gary nodded. 'He's going to bring us around on a bit of a tour, says his man is hard to find, they'll hold this for us', and he thumped the steering wheel. 'Pile of crap anyway, burning would be too good for it' and he'd focussed on Stevie, his eyes all fuzzy and glassy like he was probably higher than Stevie had thought.

And that was how it went, Gary making another call on the outskirts of the city and they'd tooled the Vectra down a narrow roadway at the back of a big hospital, cutting through the woods and a brand new Land Rover Discovery had flashed them in.

A whippet thin teenager hopped into their car as soon as they pulled the rucksack with the pump from the boot, called them 'boys' in greeting, a cigarette dangling from his lip and swung it wide on the gravel surface as a taller more muscular version stepped from the Discovery, called them 'boys' again and waved them over to the Land Rover.

They were sitting in a burger place over on the west side of the city, Gary and Stevie and Piedog the pikey, all eating chicken meals. Gary was picking at the chips but not touching the chicken and Piedog was telling them who they needed to meet.

'He's a little fucker over on the east side, Dylan, barely out of school but he's getting supplied from somewhere. Your boss knows who and he has a scatter of runners doing all the clubs'.

Gary nodded. 'And you want us to ... ease him out?' Stevie loved the way Gary talked, all laid back and cool but that was how he acted too

'Not exactly', the pikey smiled. 'We can settle him no problem, but your boss asked to let him handle it. Said it was personal, so here you are. Now are you eating that?' And he pointed at the side of charred chicken.

'We'll find him tonight and have you on the road back to Dublin by morning'. Piedog ripped the skin away, sucking on it, before digging into the white meat, wiping his mouth with the bunched-up napkin.

'The boy's will have a car at the woods when you need it', Piedog said, shovelling the last of the chips into his mouth. 'I'll use your Vectra; I wouldn't like it if you were seen in my van after this evening'.

'Van?' Gary pulled a green plastic pill bottle from his jacket pocket and shook two white pills into his palm, handed the bottle to Stevie who did the same, offered the bottle to the pikey.

'The Land Rover? My van'. Piedog refused, waved his hand. 'Naw, I never bother much anymore, selling it's enough. To tell the truth I prefer a few pints but the cops would love to bag me for that if they could', and he smiled.

'Wouldn't mind a pint or two myself', Gary nodded and that was how they ended up next-door in The High Stool, the two of them behind two pints of Guinness, Piedog nursing a large Coke.

He didn't like this, you could see it, but Tyrell had insisted. They all knew that Brando was the new supplier and that any of his buyers knocked off the block was a score for Tyrell, not to mention a message so that was why they were here. Stevie could feel the buzz building in his head, the hunger of it, the pints slipping down easy, some repeat of a Spanish football match on the flat screen, the pub cool in the evening hush.

About five they were well down the third pint and Piedog had left after an hour saying he had dogs to feed. Gary was really laid back now, the tabs chilling him and Stevie was feeling fine. He thought his eyesight was sharper, a blue tinge to the footballers, the Spanish grass greener than green, and the refs whistle loud in his ear.

'Again?' He nodded and Gary smiled his chilled smile. 'You're the driver, you're in control', and he giggled at the paraphrase of the old Therapy rock lyrics. So he called two more to the barman and squinted at the light through the coloured glass window.

There was a cut glass design set into the centre: a high stool in a stained timber finish with a little brown dog asleep between the legs of the stool. There was a coat draped on the back of the high stool and what looked like a hat, a fishing hat, resting on the bar top, a half finished pint beside it. The whole scene was saying, here is the place where you can come and have a pint after a hard day, leave your hat and coat and relax with your best friend.

Stevie snorted, his head was lightening now and he studied the other drinkers: three middle-aged guys in donkey jackets, wife fodder, holding out for the dinner. They had three pints and seemed to be engrossed in the soccer, bending with every swerve of the fleet-footed Spaniards. In the corner an old guy sat, a small whiskey on the counter before him, his face flushed and heavy with broken veins the barman keeping him in chat, not a dog or a fucken' fishing hat in sight.

The pints were settling nicely and Stevie was back in the pub on the Northside the night Gary shot Billy Butler right in the middle of the evening rush. Stevie had to do back-up that night which meant just standing inside the front door with the bike helmet still on, his hand on the butt of the pistol inside his leather jacket while Gary came through the back entrance, his helmet shiny with rain tears, a hush of purpose in how he moved, the punters pulling away as he passed, knowing in some way that death had brushed by them. Gary stopped behind Butler. Billy saw him in the big mirror and started to slide from the high stool, his hands raised, 'no, no, no', on his lips.

He would always remember how the two guys drinking with Butler had stepped back; just a step but Butler had noticed it. 'Fuckers' he cried and made to grab the barstool swinging it up like a breastplate. Gary shot him three times through the seat, the wood splintering with the first shot, the crash of the heavy handgun filling the long bar.

At the door an old man started to shuffle towards Stevie, his legs shaking, his outstretched hand trembling for the brass door handle. He'd taken one step, his hand on the butt of the pistol and the old man had frozen and Stevie had said, 'No pops. No worries, it's alright', and touched the sleeve of his worn coat, the old man standing there rocking on his old feet, blinking before he turned, trembling and found the solid wood of the bar again.

Gary straddled Butler, kicking aside the wreckage of the bar stool and fired once more, this was his signature now, the final finishing shot, a warning not to fuck, not with him. Not to fuck with those he worked for.

The barman topped the two pints off and passed them across, Gary was still slouched in the corner the brown pill bottle in his hand. Funny how the tabs made you see better, brought everything into focus.

'No pops. No worries, it's alright', Stevie muttered as he eased into the low chair and Gary smiled, repeating the mantra. 'No pops. No worries, it's alright', even pronouncing the 'alright' with an 'o' in it and they both laughed.

They'd laughed out loud in Tyrell's place when the old boy had popped up on the evening news for his famous five minutes, telling the pinch-faced correspondent how the second gunman had said, 'No pops. No worries, it's alright'. He was still trembling, his fingers picking at the frayed edge of his coat sleeve about where Stevie had touched him.

It became a bit of a catchphrase for a time after that even making the cover of one of the few political magazines, the prime-minister greeting one of his crooked business friends, an elderly tycoon in a great suit who should have been behind bars for fraud, the prime-minister smiling, and the speech bubble from his fat jowls proclaiming 'No pops. No worries, it's alright', the whole country getting the joke and knowing it was on them.

'Time to be going so', Piedog was behind them and Gary lifted the rucksack with the pump inside from between his legs, drained the Guinness and they followed him out.

The Vectra was parked near the bottle bank and Piedog insisted that they both travel in the back. 'Less chance of been seen, more chance to see', was how he put it. They eased into the flow and Stevie was surprised how snarled it was.

'Always this way on a Friday', Piedog nodded. 'Everyone out for the shopping', and he eased up behind a people-carrier, mum, dad and the kids.

They were crossing the river, still nose to tail when Piedog muttered under his breath, 'fuck, fuck', and tapped the brakes.

'Wha?' Gary shook himself. 'Wha'?'

'Dylan! There he is, the little fucker'. Piedog pointed ahead through the traffic crawl.

'Where?' Stevie had difficulty focussing, the footpaths heavy with people.

'Dylan. There, anorak and the bike, talking to the young doll, pushing it, see'. And sure enough there he was, a tall skinny guy with a scraggy ponytail and a long, flappy coat, pushing a battered mountain bike.

'Fuck, fuck!' Piedog was punching the rim of the steering wheel.

'Relax man', Gary was rummaging in the rucksack, pulling a pair of sunglasses and a baseball cap from one of the side pockets.

'Here', he tossed a woolly hat across. 'Roll it and don't pull it down until we're on him'. Stevie stared at the hat.

'We're going to do it here? Now?'

'Why not? Let him walk a little, see where he's going and if we get a chance, do it'.

'No, no!' Piedog was adamant. 'The traffic is too heavy, look we're crawling, no way'.

'Relax I said'. He'd seen Gary like this before, it was like a chiller kicked in; he could plan on the hoof, decide in a second and never call it wrong.

The cyclist was chatting to a tall, dark-haired girl in a leather jacket and tight jeans. They weren't gaining on him, the lights holding them up. They watched as he leant in and pecked her cheek and she nipped up a narrow side street, the cyclist continuing on, still pushing the bicycle.

'What street is that?' Gary pointed as the cyclist turned the corner.

'Merchants' Road, it's busy but at least he won't recognise the van'.

'The van. What van?'

'This van', Piedog glared at Gary. 'I'll pull in here until we see what he does'. He swung the Vectra onto a grid of yellow lines behind a Quasqai outside a tall apartment building.

'Maybe we should wait?' Stevie wasn't so sure now; the Guinness was clouding him, the pills still forcing the focus.

'We are waiting'. This from Gary.

The cyclist sauntered along apparently without too many cares, the long coat flapping, like he thought he was safe in daylight. Then he swung across through the traffic which seemed to be getting lighter, some cars filtering left towards the city centre and man-handled the bike against the railings.

'He's locking it, the careful little fucker'. This from Gary. 'What's he at?'

'I know! I know!' Piedog was leaning forward. 'He's doing a drop for Moley'.

'Moley?'

'Yeah, one of his runners lives in a flat on the Dockside, student, he does the clubs and he's going to use the rat run'.

'Rat run?' Gary again, he was getting tired of all the questions, Stevie could hear it in his voice.

'Watch'. And sure enough the cyclist sauntered along the footpath and seemed to vanish between two tall buildings.

'C'mon', Piedog put the Vectra in gear and they edged forward. Sure enough a narrow walkway appeared to their right paved in brick and wide enough for two people, which led through to the next street.

Piedog smiled. 'The little fucker has to come back the same way to get back to the bike!'

Gary cackled. 'We'll do him then'.

'Are you sure?' Piedog still wasn't convinced.

'Yes, I'm sure'. Gary was checking the pump, feeding shells into the chamber.

'Fuck, what does that thing hold?' Piedog stared.

'Eight. Should be enough'. Gary pumped the first shell into the chamber before he slipped the shotgun, barrel first back into the rucksack.

'Can you meet us on the other street?' Gary was thinking now.

'Not a bother, I'll even let you know when he's coming and all you have to do is continue on through, turn left and I'll be parked there. We'll be on the Lake Road and out the wood in five minutes. The traffic's getting light'. The pikey seemed more up for it now.

They were browsing the window of the Chandler's shop, wondering at the variety and the colours of the waterproof clothing, the giant model of a yacht, a large plastic gull eyeing them from a rope display in the corner when Gary's phone purred.

'We're on', he nodded. 'Off you go'. Stevie settled the rucksack carefully on his left shoulder, Gary giving it a quick tug to make sure it was settled, 'ok, ok', and he was off. The traffic had lightened to almost nothing, a slow trickle and he crossed easily to the entrance to the alleyway.

The cyclist seemed to have just entered the alleyway from the other end. Stevie could feel the chemicals buzzing in his head, the sky still too blue, a vertical slice of it, with one mast like a giant finger pointing, the cyclist loping towards him.

Stevie could see him taking the situation in, 'student' he probably thought, rucksack, 'definitely student'. Then he could hear Gary coming, his blur of language calling loud into the mobile phone.

'Naw, naw, I told you Julie, naw it's all wrong, you'll have to start again'. He could see Gary in his mind's eye almost looking into the mobile phone in anger. 'Naw, you have to use steak, steak, not mince Julie. Mince is fucken useless ...'

Gary was coming up fast and there was a hint of confusion on the face of the cyclist. He was focussing on Gary's gab, not even looking at Stevie any longer. He felt Gary's hand grab the rounded ball of the stock, the pump sliding from the rucksack, the mobile phone hitting the cobbles, the boom of the first shell lifting the cyclist off his feet, the 'uh' as the lead parcel hit him square in the chest. Then Gary was past him, jacking another shell into the chamber, the cyclist looking down, open-mouthed at the mess on his chest and the second shell took his face away.

'Get the phone! Get the shells!' Gary was calling as he straddled the body. He fired once more, the shell ejecting against the brick and he bent and scooped it almost before it stopped spinning, Stevie unrolling the woolly hat into a mask, Gary pulling the baseball hat low and slipping on the dark glasses and they were running.

No one entered the alleyway. They exited at speed and turned left, they kept the disguises on. You couldn't take chances. You just couldn't be sure.

'Who is Julie? Stevie had to ask.

'Fucked if I know, but she can't cook', Gary gasped. 'He seemed to like her'.

'Where's the pikey?' Stevie shouted, the Vectra nowhere to be seen.

'Fuck, fuck', Gary was running ahead. 'The fucker's legged it, fucker!' People were turning to look at them, not really taking a great interest, thinking students, out on the piss, even with the balaclava and the sunglasses.

They were coming to a set of lights and Gary was going spare. 'I'll fucken do him if it takes me ten, I'll do him'.

'Boys'. They both jumped, Piedog stood behind them at the entrance to a side street. 'Are we ready so?'

Gary gave a tight laugh, 'we thought you'd legged it'.

Piedog was already walking to the Vectra, his trainers soundless on the dry pavement. They hopped into the rear seats and now that it was over Stevie could feel the sweat break, his whole body like pins and needles, and a pulse popping in the back of his left leg, just behind the knee.

'Is it sorted?' Piedog put the Vectra into gear and exited the mouth of the narrow street. They were still on Merchants Road but well beyond the entrance to the alleyway. A few cars had stopped and people were straining for a look. No sign of any cops yet so they were well away.

'Steady now boys and we'll be out the road in no time. Let's not fuck it up now'. Piedog straightened himself and sat well back in the seat. Stevie swung the rucksack from behind him, easing the pump from the open top and rested it across his knees. Gary leant towards him; his eyes were pin-point bright and burning.

'Never knew what hit him, did you see the look on his face? Fucker'. Gary laughed again; there were beads of sweat on his forehead. 'Jesus it's hot in here'.

Piedog hit a button on the console. The passenger window slid open and a rush of cold air hit them head on.

'Fuck that's good'. Stevie hefted the pump, it felt heavy now. He loved the way the rounded butt settled into his palm, his heart was racing too, the dealer lifting, hitting the brick wall again and again in his mind's eye. Ahead of them the traffic was backing up a little but the main flow was heading towards the city. Piedog glanced in the rear-view mirror, nodded.

'Lights. We're fine once we get through these'. He was smiling, happy at a job done; Tyrell would be pleased, the war going on. Stevie curled his index finger around the trigger, feeling the slight pull, the raw power of it. He could see the pikey watching him in the mirror.

'Careful there Stevie', Gary touched his arm. 'We don't need an accident now'.

'Relax', Stevie smiled, pushing the pump between the front seats. 'We're the very best'. He'd get Flick back even if she ran. He would.

'Yeah, fucking right', Gary was leaning back, his head against the headrest, his eyes unfocussed. 'No pops. No worries, it's alright', he giggled, wiping his hand across his mouth. They were easing up to the traffic lights, Stevie still pressed forward between the front seats.

'You should have seen it', he said again to the pikey. 'Lifted the fucker ten foot in the air'. He could see it in his mind's eye, the power of it and the rush of air by his cheek as Gary fired.

Piedog was trying to keep his eye on the traffic but Stevie could see that his mind was on the shotgun. He could see him shift and Stevie liked it, he jiggled the weapon a little, lifting the barrel off the seat. The pikey was worried; he could see it, easing up to the lights, three or four cars ahead of him and the lights on red.

'Careful with that', the pikey nodded, Stevie looked at Gary and giggled again.

'Fuck!' Piedog muttered. A white Transit was trying to cross the line of traffic to exit right on to College Road. 'What the fuck are you doing?' He called, the driver of the van pointing frantically.

'Fucker'. Piedog hit the brakes, the white van squeezing him, the driver had dropped the window fully now, leaning out, calling something.

Stevie pushed his head and shoulders between the seats, the headrest hampering him. 'What? ... He asked. 'What's your problem?' his face to the open window.

'Back up a little willya and let me through, good lad' the driver called.

'D'ya hear this fucker? Good lad?' he nodded to Gary. 'Just listen to him'.

He felt a sudden surge of rage, everyone telling him something, Tyrell, Gary, Flick. The smug look on the driver's face as he kept pushing in.

The tilt was minimal before he squeezed the trigger, the boom of the pump in the closed-in space, the violent kick, the driver screaming as the heavy load hit him.

'Christ, ya little fucker'. Piedog roared. 'Ya stupid cunt!'

Stevie watched the driver slump against the steering wheel of the Transit, one side of his face a mottled mush of tissue and flesh, the Transit nudging gently into the side of the Vectra.

'Ya stupid little fucker!' Piedog screamed again and Gary leant forward and eased the pump from Stevie's locked grip.

'I told you before not to play with guns Stephen', he said, jacking the spent shell from the pump and ramming the barrel into the back of Piedog's neck. 'Now, drive pikey', he whispered. 'Drive like your whole life depends on it'.

Building a Small World

'Robbie's sick', was how my sister put it and I knew she wasn't talking flu or anything like it. We'd been separated for about five years but I'd never bothered getting it sorted, he'd pay what he could when he could and after Desmond died I didn't see the need. There was no need then.

Her husband had heard it at a darts match the week before in some pub behind the river, someone's hand offered for the sad news and he'd played it out, pretending his own knowledge until he could read the territory and then he called to see Robbie the next day.

I'd known for weeks that something was up without anyone saying it, just the way people looked at me, the unsaid pity of it, the angled enquiries here and there, the turned-away glance, the captured stare. I'd done nothing about it, how could I? But when she called to the house, the same hidden look around her eyes I remembered from when we were children, I knew whatever she asked for she'd get it.

So I'd taken the railway path to town, a little time to take it all in, looking out over the whipping green of the bay, the thunder of the wind in my ears, the gulls holding on and holding on before breaking for the waves, coming in low, their cries pleading.

He had a single room back near the fire station, his name above a battered bell, but he was doing no work, maybe the odd small account, a hurried tax-return, the button painted over in a dulled grey, the colour of misery. I could hear him coming well before he pulled the door open, the rattled wheeze and the scrape of the door.

Maybe my sister should have warned me, I wasn't ready. The suit hung off him like a peg, his neck channelled, thin, the shirt too big for him, his eyes burning out of the yellowing skull.

What could I do after that? I sat and watched the brittle shake of his hand on the whiskey glass as he told me, the doctor's words pressing him down, his eyes to the golden glow.

I hadn't had a drink myself in over two years but I could have taken one then. I made a cup of tea instead, clearing the clutter from the sink, finding a clean cup towards the back of the press.

'It won't be long', was how he put it and I'd started gathering his few things into a black sack: shirts with stained collars, the jacket of a suit, and I don't know why, a second pair of shoes. The taxi dropped us at the front door and I made him a cup of tea, sat him staring by the fireplace, nothing there but ashes, while I sheeted the bed in the spare room. I heard the clink of the naggin bottle as he added heat to the cup while I smoothed the creases, made the angles good.

He stopped at the door of Desmond's room when I helped him upstairs but I keep it closed. There's nothing in there now so he turned left for the bathroom, the shower on hot, a new towel on the low chair.

'Leave your things outside', I told him. 'I'll deal with them later'.

'Thanks Kathy'. His voice was husky and he tried to take my wrist but I handed him the clean pyjamas and moved ahead.

The police never brought Desmond home they came for me instead. He'd been missing for three days by then and I was getting worried; Desmond could be like that but three days was very long. I knew it wasn't good when I pulled the door open and saw them there, Robbie slouched by the garden gate.

'No!' Was all I could manage, repeating it to Robbie as he moved up the path, his arms spread wide. The two guards moved aside and I hit him, hard across the face before they could stop me, straining to get at him, the young policeman holding me back.

They were brief in their explanations, the guards, sitting at the kitchen table, the younger man between us and they told us what they had. Desmond had been found behind the football pitches, wrapped in an old sleeping bag, his hands were tied and he'd been shot.

I had to pull for detail and after the shock all you can do is ask.

'I want to know everything', I explained to the older man, Robbie pacing the kitchen floor, his head down.

'There's very little', the older man explained. 'They're doing tests now and the pitches are closed off'.

'I want to see, take me there'.

'No Kathy', Robbie stopped. But I insisted, taking my coat from the tall press.

The tent looked smaller than you'd see on TV, too small to cover a life, even a short one, just a white rectangle, flimsy, sitting at an angle to the scrubby slope. Someone had cut the bushes back and the police pointed out the digger tracks in the muddy earth.

'They'd never have found him if they hadn't started clearing. The driver saw the bundle and got down to check'.

Three men in white overalls and masks moved around, entering and leaving the tent and taking photographs. There was a silence like I'd never felt before, just hanging there, holding on like something else might happen yet.

'Is Desmond in there now?' I had to know.

'No. We moved him before we called to your house'. The policeman was trying to be gentle.

'Where?'

'I'll take you', and he looked to Robbie who stood on the slope, his back to us, wiping his eyes as he turned.

I look at him now lying in the single bed, his neck wattled against the blue pyjama top, his head barely denting the pillow and I recall him when we were first married. He'd never played any sport but he still bought a pair of running shoes, they were all the rage then and he was gaining weight.

'I'm going to start by walking', he smiled. 'Two miles on Sunday as far as Merlin Park and two miles back'. And that was what we did, making for the Dublin Road, we were living in the town then, and we walked.

After about a mile the shoes began to tighten, the uppers stiff with newness but we kept going. It wasn't until we were passing the cemetery that I saw the shadows at his heels, the blisters had begun to weep but he shrugged it off.

'A blister or two never killed anyone', he laughed and we walked all the way there and even then he wouldn't hear of taking the bus back. The last mile home must have been agony, he rolled his steps to keep it eased but he still kept going. When we reached the house I had to soak his feet in a basin of warm water and ease the socks away from the torn flesh, the blood turning the water pink.

I see him now, barely propped, his hand drifting to the glass, no distance at all and yet he can't control it. No distance worth measuring and yet the pain is greater than a walk to the cemetery and he catches me watching him and he looks away.

I stopped drinking myself that day I saw Desmond on the trolley, a hush in the cold, marbled room, the policeman clearing his throat like a gunshot, the white walls echoing.

'Is this your son, Desmond King?' And I stared and stared, the life gone out of him, his ribcage a wicker of criss-crossed blues, his nails broken back like he'd clung on to the world as they'd dragged him, no back to his shaven head.

'Yes'. I looked at Robbie there beside me, his stare fixed to the face. I touched his arm and he shook his head.

'It's not Desmond'.

The policeman looked confused, glanced at his colleague, frowning.

'Mister King I need a formal identification. Is this your son, Desmond King?'

'No'. His voice was stronger this time. I turned to the policeman.

'It is. This is Desmond King'.

'But ...'

I looked at Robbie and he looked away. 'You know this is Desmond, you know it Robbie'.

'It can't be', he whispered. 'It can't be him. I won't let it!'

At that the policeman nodded and made a note on a clipboard and eased the cloth over my son's questioning face.

I didn't pour it down the sink. Instead I took the tins and the few bottles I hadn't touched to the bottle-bank by the Sports Centre and listened to each heavy thud as the full cans landed, the tinkle of the bursting whiskey bottles, and the catching waft of malt floating upwards on the tingling air. Then I stopped at the church. I have no faith left but I like the quiet and how it helps me think and I sat.

The day of Desmond's funeral the place was full, locals mostly and a lot of Desmond's friends. I prefer the people who say nothing; because they know it can't be said. But they take your hand and hold it, I can manage that. During the homily I watched his friends sectioned near the coffin in dark clothes, boys and girls all together and I wondered if one of them had done it, and why? We'd never know and time has proved me right, more of them gone since with newer faces every day.

One lad came to me outside the church afterwards, the crowds milling, carrying me away from Desmond, away from the hearse. He pressed my hand, this lad barely Desmond's age and whispered, 'It won't end here, Mrs King'. I could see him on that same trolley as clear as day and I shook my head and pleaded but I knew he wouldn't listen.

After the funeral I never saw Robbie for a year. He came with the money once but we didn't talk. My sister kept me up to date on roughly when he finally lost his job. The while he did the books for some crooked businessman on the docks. How close he came to dying or being beaten up when some Polish lads weren't paid. It all filtered back; even if it's not said it always filters back.

Pity has its uses and I made it work, building a small world for myself. The local shop took me on a day a week at first, the manager uncomfortable with my cold hand but now I'm up to four and weekends too and I use the money wisely, the curtains are new and the carpets grip the corners, the garden full of flowers. I have my rituals and I hold to them, the house is clean, a long walk in the evenings, a film that takes me away. Books.

I go into Desmond's room from time to time, no ritual there. It's easy to keep it clean, I stroke his clothes, fix the odd poster on the bedroom wall, and move a discarded hoodie or a pair of jeans from here to there, conjure up the semblance of occupation.

When Robbie was home about two weeks the doctor and the hospice nurse began to call, they gave him the option of home or away. It was time. It had to be his choice, I'd go with that.

'I'll stay if that's alright, Kathy?'

He was in bed all the time now, all the day-to-day behind him, a shrunken presence making the single bed look big.

'He'll have no pain', the doctor promised. 'We'll see to that and he's happy here'. Happy was hardly the correct word but I knew what he meant. It wouldn't be long more.

I took to sitting with him. The room was golden that final evening, his breathing barely there. I'd wait with him now. A whisper of pain crossed his face and it was a second or two before I realised his eyes were open. His hand moved on the cold duvet as he touched mine. He wanted to speak, I could feel it. I leant closer, his voice a spent echo.

'I've always loved you Kathy', his eyes probing. I could see the question.

'I love you Kathy'.

He waited. A rain cloud covered the sun, I held his hand and I waited and said nothing. I waited until the room was almost in total darkness and he was gone. Then the light from the bay filled the bedroom again and in the glow his colour settled and he looked more like the Robbie I used to know before time overtook him, overtook us both and pushed us all off course.

BOTTLE

They were discussing what women want the morning when the text came through. The facilitator was leading them through the maze of her own thinking, explaining that they really were standing at the edge of a giant forest and here she smiled.

'There's a path leading in, but it isn't much'.

Jenny sneaked a quick peek, thinking it might be Greg, but found her mother instead. 'Text me when you're free and I'll phone you. Love, Mum'.

'The auctioneer has come back to me'. Her mother sounded upset, but that wasn't unusual either. She lived on the east coast down towards Bray, had done for years. She was more than a little surprised when Jenny had opted for her post-grad work in the west and since Jenny's father had died she had so little to do it even worried Jenny.

'You know how your aunt Betty and myself talked about selling the place down there and buying a little house in Portugal. Well, we're going ahead'. Jenny could sense her mother's firmness even down the phone. This was it, her mother's next, newest sense of purpose.

'Yes, mum'. Jenny was well used to this particular conversation. She'd had versions of it during the year and she'd even checked the farmhouse a few times since she'd arrived, just to keep her mother happy, but it was a chore. Greg and Moley stood in the background; Greg was making match-striking gestures and pretending to puff flames. He thought her mother was a dragon.

'Well', and here her mother paused. 'He wants almost fifteen hundred euro to clear out the house. He thinks someone might buy it for renovation now, what with the price drops and everything. He says a skip will cost over four hundred euro and then there's two men for two days as well ... and he wants another thousand euro for that. Imagine, a thousand euro, I think it's disgraceful and at the present time too ...'

'But mum ...'

Her mother wasn't finished, 'I was thinking Jenny, maybe you could get a few of your friends ...'

Jenny interrupted, 'You want me to get someone to do it?'

'No dear, I was thinking that maybe Greg and one or two ...' She knew Greg, 'Maybe he could get a few friends to empty it out and the furniture is finished anyway'.

'Greg?' Greg was making faces now and hiding behind Moley gesturing. 'Greg is very busy studying mum; he has exams in less than three months'. Jenny turned away trying to keep serious.

'I'd pay him of course and his friends. I don't expect it for nothing. You could rent the skip there and say ... three hundred euro for Greg and whoever helps'.

'Three hundred euro?' Greg had stopped teasing now and was pointing at his chest, mouthing, 'me, me?'

'Yes dear, three hundred and the cost of the skip. That would mean I'd get it done for half what Shanaghan wants'.

'OK mum, Greg is in the Department now, I'll talk to him but if he can't, he can't. You'll have to go with Shanaghan's price'.

They were locked in, her thin muscular stomach to his, the slap, slap of his plunges filling her as he pumped and she could hear her own cry building and the mobile phone purred and purred on the bedside locker and she locked her arms around his shoulders, her cry drowning it out and they were both lost to the chime as the message followed, lost to the cold room and the rushing traffic in the street outside.

'Fuck it! I'll do it!' Greg scratched his mop of curls. 'I'll do it, but she has to stop phoning and texting and always at the wrong time!'

'Greg!'

They were caught in a tangle of duvet and bottom sheet, legs entwined and Jenny stripped the last of the orange peel, split the segments and fed two into Greg's mouth. Moley had gone back to his own place; before he'd left he'd agreed that it was a good gig. They could always use three hundred euro, even if Moley was rarely short of money.

'Are you sure? I know that it's €300 but who else would you get, Quickpic?

'Hey it's three hundred euro and with College Week coming up it's a no-brainer. So yes, it's Moley and Quickpic to the rescue'.

Quickpic turned up with a short axe he'd found in his landlord's garage and Moley had a massive sledgehammer. He said he'd found it lying on the quayside one night when the trawlers had put out into the bay. Almost tripped over it as he made his way home from some club, and he tipped a wink at Jenny.

'Couldn't leave it there', he mused. 'Someone might have stolen it'. Quickpic also had a dozen tins of cider, the plastic slab looking sturdy, and solid, slightly tilted on the back seat.

'Now, where's this house we have to demolish?' Quickpic joked as they piled into the Punto, the upholstery hinting of vomit and strong weed.

They moved through the cobwebbed kitchen squeezing between the angled clutter of furniture. Soot had leaked from the cracked chimney-breast, a sour stain on the peeling wall, a catching tang in the back of the throat, a dusty, unoccupied tickle in the nostrils.

'What a shithole!' This from Moley and he swung the sledgehammer against a timber box the head passing through the side in a splintering dust.

'Fuck Moley, you're such a wrecker'. Quickpic was skinning a thin one, his nose close to the rollie as he trickled the tobacco weed mix in a thin worm the length of the paper.

'Fuckoff ya skinny fucker'. Moley swung the sledge again. More dust.

Jenny could never be sure what Quickpic thought of the taller, scruffy student. Moley was 'completing' a Masters in something Mathematical and designing board games for children on the side, but the College had just terminated his funding, so she wondered. Some people hinted that he was selling highs but she'd never seen it and Jenny thought he was working hard. But he went to the clubs most nights, even nights when the rest of them stayed at home and worked and he always had money.

Greg came pushing through from the bedroom, the tattered skeleton of a broom held high ahead of him, knocking cobwebs from the ceiling, a black lacework of soot and dust settling on their shoulders, filling their nostrils.

'Let's start by putting all this shite in the garden. We've no skip until Jenny gets the cash from her mother. Get everything out and then we can load the skip'. He was enjoying this, Jenny could see it. Cobwebs clung to him and he'd tied a bandanna around his head, his hair poking through which gave him a distinctly Spanish look as he drained the can.

'Ok, let's take a room each'. Quickpic was sorted now, pinching the roll-up. 'I'll take this bedroom', he eased around the kitchen furniture, had a look. 'Yes, this will do me fine. Let's go!'

'Fine, I'll take the other bedroom', Moley hefted the sledgehammer. 'Which leaves this beautiful airy space for the two of you', and he smiled at Greg and Jenny.

Quickpic had started by heaving the remains of a double bed outside to flatten the weeds, dragging the mattress like a pup with a blanket, growling. Jenny and Greg took a small chest between then and manhandled it through the backdoor before dropping it in the tall grass. Quickpic was poking a mound of rags by the corner of the shed.

'I'd say you might have a tenant', he pointed. 'Looks like a sleeping bag'.

Greg hoisted it high by one corner, smeared tissues and a crumpled can falling from the open mouth.

'Shit, looks like a mess. I'd say it's been here a while'. He shook it again.

'Toss it on the heap', Quickpic pointed. 'We'll get rid of it later'.

After that they'd emptied steadily, broken chairs, dressing tables, some sort of a washstand which was almost totally disintegrated, the dowels separating, the frame buckled.

'For washing yer bollocks', Moley confided. 'I saw it on TV, there's supposed to be a basin and a jug as well'. He swung a leg and squatted to demonstrate. 'See, you did it like this', and Quickpic shoved, Moley toppling across it, the stand crumpling to nothing at all, Quickpic darting away, laughing.

By the afternoon there were little mounds of furniture and rubbish dotted around the garden and the house was beginning to look empty and more manageable.

'Your mother collected a lot of shit rubbish'. Greg was struggling with the dresser which had collapsed on one side, the boards rotted to a brown mush.

'It's not all hers, her dad lived here and his father before that and who knows who else? I even came on holidays here sometimes when he was still alive' Jenny was clearing the windowsills, putting all the little bits into an old plastic bucket, small glass ornaments, egg-cups, three rusted metal stumps on the mantelpiece behind one of the leaning candlesticks, a memory flickered of her grandfather rattling them in his calloused palm.

Greg was struggling with the dresser. 'This thing is absolutely rotten, look!' He pulled one of the shelves which gave with a creak. Jenny came to stand beside him, a box rested high on the top shelf. She took it down and attempted to open it.

'Gimme'. Greg struggled with the lid, the rust holding it tight. Finally it gave, the pin hinges separating and the lid dropping to the floor. A bundle of musty paper had slipped to one end of the tin, Greg turned it over.

'Pictures!' He lifted the hoard, easing them apart, spreading them on the lower shelf.

'Look, Americans!' And he turned the faded picture of a large American car towards her, four figures lined up before it in a firing-squad formation, posing.

'And look, it's you!' He exclaimed, flicking another photo, pointing to one of the two girls their arms around the shoulders of an older woman. 'And your mother too!'

'Fuckoff, it's not even in colour!' Jenny took the picture, there was definitely a resemblance, and the girl on the left looked familiar. She turned the rectangle of thin card but the writing had faded to almost nothing.

'I know. That's my mother here and this must be my aunt Betty and that's my gran. I don't remember her at all'.

'Your gran?'

'Yes, my other gran, she died before I was born; I only ever had one gran'.

'Lazy fuckers, get a move on'. Moley eased through from the garden. 'Quickpic thinks we should burn the lot. No need for a skip, way more money for beer'.

'What!' Jenny stared. This was a new turn.

'Think about it. You're waiting for your mum to transfer the money; it would be easier to burn it'.

'Seven hundred for beer', Greg's voice sounded wistful. 'Sounds like a plan Jen. This would be an amazing College Week'.

Jenny turned towards him, he sounded different, like this was really important.

'She'll notice, won't she? I mean, won't there be ashes?'

'Tell her we filled the skip and had to burn the rest ... Simple!' Greg smiled.

Jenny wasn't sure; she didn't want to upset Greg.

'Well it seems like a waste of good money, that's all'. And he spread his hands.

'Yep, I hate waste', and Moley turned back to the garden.

They stood in the fading stillness surveying their evening's work. The space was dotted with small piles of rubbish, everything from stacks of holy pictures to old wardrobes and peeling mirrors, mottled reflections everywhere.

'We could build a fire there, toss on the bits gradually and have a barbeque of all this shit'. Moley pulled the old mattress a little further away from the backdoor.

'We could?' Greg glanced sideways at Jenny knowing it was her call.

'Ok, but let's be careful, let's keep the fire manageable'. Jenny had a buzzing in her head, three cans of cider wasn't a lot, maybe it was all the work, and she'd sweated as well.

'We'll need petrol', Quickpic smiled, ever the science student. 'Nothing like a good accelerant'.

'Bollocks!'

'Ok. You try to light some of this shit. I have a plastic can; I'll nip down to the garage'.

'And get another slab of cider', Moley added, slipping twenty from his pocket. 'This furniture moving makes me thirsty'.

They were still struggling with the dresser when Quickpic got back, a blue plastic container in one hand and the slab of cider in the other. He made a great show of cracking another can before throwing his weight behind the dresser as they tilted it on its side, easing it through the backdoor, leaving a black scar in the weeds as they pushed.

'Ok, let's get started', Moley was dousing the mattress with the petrol, sprinkling it wide and rummaging in his jeans for a lighter.

'Stand back!' He spread his arms like a master of ceremonies and they were all laughing as he touched the lighter to a twist of paper. The sudden crump made them jump slightly as the flames shot up.

'Fuck! Did you use the lot?' Quickpic giggled, the heat burning their faces.

Moley was laughing and examining his arm. 'Yeah!' Most of the hair was gone and there was singed smell.

'Let's get this stuff on!' Greg tossed the remains of a chair and Moley grabbed the sledge and splintered a dressing table. Then everything speeded up, Quickpic pulled the car closer, opened the boot lid and tuned the player to some ultimate clubbing station, loud. Moley was attacking the dresser, the sledge sinking into the soft wood, Quickpic swinging the axe as it sliced through the shelves.

Jenny felt as if she didn't belong somehow, the boys were so focussed on this one thing. She looked at Greg, he came running from the house, a large plaster virgin held high above his head and tossed it to the flames. 'There she goes', he roared. 'Ireland's last virgin!' Then he turned and began chucking the holy pictures on the fire. 'And all the fucking saints as well!'

Jenny watched the faces of the saints darken behind the smoked glass, the virgin sinking slowly into the centre of the blaze, the blue of her long gown fading. Greg swung the sleeping bag they'd found earlier above his head, swinging it like a magic carpet before releasing it and it landed with a dull sag, smothering half the fire.

'More wood! More wood!' Moley shouted, hefting one of the dressing tables high in the smoky air and tossing it, sparks showering them and they piled on more and more, the blaze building, the cider cutting the smoke and ash from their parched throats. Their energy was making her tired.

Jenny was resting on the chest and thumbing through the contents of the old box. Her history was here, she recognised her mother in several pictures and her grand-dad too. She found a picture of him on his own, hat firmly in place. He was a vague memory but she still smiled. She remembered that look her mum called 'jaunty', the word came back to her, she still missed him. Sometimes you needed a small key to open a big lock. Holiday thoughts came to her, 'easy-time' her dad had called it.

He was standing beside them before they noticed. Greg was hunkered down at the rim of the fire staring into the flames, a can in one hand and Quickpic was helping Moley who was poking a burning wardrobe, pushing it deeper into the flames. He turned, tossing the sledgehammer, it landed almost at the feet of the ragged figure flickering in the firelight. His face was streaked with blood and one eye was swollen closed.

'What the fuck are you all doing?' He was angry, his finger pointing.

'Moley and Greg moved closer together, Quickpic took a step back.

'Relax man', Moley smiled. 'What's your problem?'

The wino was a little older than themselves, maybe mid-twenties, with a shaven head. At some stage his nose had been broken and he had a wild, almost frenzied look. He swung the bottle, sloshing wine on his wrist.

'Problem? What problem? You have the problem'. He took a step towards them.

'Relax man, it's not a problem'. Moley glanced at Greg.

'I sleep here. This is my place. Now fuck off'.

Jenny studied the confrontation, placing the photographs carefully in the box.

'No this is my place', she cried, leaving the tin on a flat stone, the cider making her brave. 'My mother owns it!'

'Why don't you live here then?' The wino screamed. ''I'll tell you why, 'cos I live here'. He wiped the blood from his cheek. 'Fuckers!'

'Now look', Greg blustered. 'This is Jenny's place. She's at college here, we all are'.

'Fucking students. Scabbing bastards!' He drank from the wine bottle, draining it. Then his gaze seemed to settle on the fire.

'My bag', he cried. 'That's my sleeping bag'. He bent deliberately and jabbed the empty wine bottle against the head of the discarded sledgehammer, swung upwards without warning and caught Moley along the thigh with the jagged end. Moley screamed and collapsed backwards his hand clamping the wound, Quickpic trying to hold him. Then the wino turned his attention to Greg, weaving the broken bottle before his face. Greg took a step back, the fire roaring behind him, Quickpic bending to help Moley.

Jenny felt the handle of the short axe in her hand; the bottle glinted, the burning prisms flashing light. She felt the silence as she swung, the flat of the axe catching the wino high across the back, the bottle dropping from his grip, almost no sound as he crumpled, Greg, Moley and Quickpic frozen in the blazing tableau.

The wino groaned and tried to rise but she dropped to her knees beside him, swung the axe again the blade sinking in the remains of the wooden shelf by his head. He gasped, scrabbling on the slippery grass.

'Now, whose place is this?' Jenny whispered, his stare on the blade as she pulled it free.

'Yours, it's yours!' He jumped to his feet and hobbled away to disappear into the darkness.

Jenny turned without speaking and pointed towards the open boot lid of the Punto, holding their stares, the music still booming.

'Maybe we could turn that down a little?'

She took the box from the flat stone and shuffled to sit on the wooden chest again, smiled into the flames, drew the old box closer.

1927: Hat

We were standing at one of the new gates leading to the far fields and my father, John was rubbing the ball of his thumb along the silvered edge of the severed bolt.

My seven year old certainties were telling me exactly who had done the damage, their bitterness reflected in the polished end of the bolt, the hacked-off stump of it lying in the stubble, the filings still fresh on the packed earth.

'We'll check the others so', he said, pushing the gate closed and rolling a stone from the wall against the bottom bar. My father had just finished fitting three new gates to our fields, the pillars built from stones and sweating sea sand; they would ooze for years. But he'd drawn the stones himself, hauled the sand from the shore, mixed the cement with Mack Harty and they'd shuttered the lot in off-cuts of old timber.

The pillars had stood empty for months, the first and the straightest in the townland, the thick steel pins ready to take the weight, until he'd paid the blacksmith for the three new, iron gates, hammered from salvaged wheel hoops and slotted them in on the upright poles, bedding each upright in the metal 'spud', swinging them easy on a bed of grease, driving the sturdy bolts home.

The other two gates were exactly the same, the bolts sheared off, the filings like fresh silver, the stumps discarded where they'd fallen.

'I'd say something now if I had them locked', he smiled, rattling the three sheared bolt-ends in his calloused palm. These were the years just after the Civil War, still a time of low-level skirmishes, simmering hatreds and the civility of cracked heads. The war was over, our family split up and my father had returned to farming fulltime, the gun buried, his younger brother Pat abroad to keep ahead of the new police.

We turned towards the house, one of the ten or so in the village, sloping towards the bay, the tide rolling in, my mother pinning sheets in the apple-garden, the salt-sharp air whipping them high and away from her stretching hands.

'We won't upset your mother now' was how he put it. 'I'll tell her in my own time'.

He never repaired the severed bolts, leaving them for time to heal the hacked scars and a week later the three severed ends appeared on the mantelpiece above the polished range, three metal soldiers upright before the mirror, steel bullets to kill the ghosts in my child's mind and I would have used them on 'The Bowler', in my head anyway, if I'd had the knowhow or the buried gun.

So I was seven in twenty-seven and the man from the government came visiting Lar Feeney's sister, carrying his bulk well along the narrow road in a long dark greatcoat and a bowler hat.

'That's a bloody strange hat, John' was how Mack Harty put it to my father. 'Or are we living in a Free State or what?'

'The land-agent's hat?' My father smiled. And I stood between them looking up into their broad farming faces and wishing that I could grasp the reasons behind their sudden smiles, the hidden reasons, their crinkled, wise eyes.

Maybe I learned that year as well how narrow trust could be, how controlled it all was, how the eyes and ears were shared by everyone, the inching church, the neighbours, the new police, a shared conscience keeping it aloft, sealed in, a looming fear holding it all in place.

'It's a bowler hat, Mack, that's all. There's a lot worse than that going around'.

And he was right, of course. It was a hat not seen very often anymore this far south but a hat none-the-less and the government man wore it well on his well-groomed head, walking the three miles from the town. The rumour was he was a widower, lately come to grief, and had children and needs. He had a job in the new government, which we all hated, somewhere in the middle between boss and minion and he had a little power.

He'd taken a shine to Feeney's sister, neither of them young, the boat already sailed, but Lar Feeney was happy to go to the pub in the evening, his mother safely there to attend to all, to mind the family name, everyone happy with the arrangement except that is for my suffering mother.

'He's turning our pillar green the dirty bastard!' This was how my mother put it that day when she thought I was safely out of range. 'The dirty bugger's pissing on our gate, using it as a toilet, why doesn't he piss at her house. She knows him well enough by now I'm sure'.

'He's a dirty bastard right enough!' Harty exclaimed, smiling at the buried hint, pushing his sweaty hat to the back of his bald head and slapping the threshing table with his hand. He knew where he was talking, my father's friends sweat-cooled and easy sitting there with the floating motes hanging in the shafted sunlight, the chaff crusting on their heavy boots.

'He should know better, working for the government and all, with a good coat and a bowler hat, he should know better'. This from Josie Burke who rarely said anything at all and could sit for hours almost motionless, a thin cigarette smouldering between his fingers, his attention moving from face to face, following the conversation, the tea cup lost in his huge grip.

'The Bowler' was all they called him after that and when he didn't stop my father had no choice but to wait and warn him one night, though it meant standing between the looming stacks in the haggard dark, a hammered copper moon throwing whetted outlines you could feel along the straw-littered ground.

I can remember there, my small hand inside his calloused one. My mother had sent me in my thin cotton shirt to tell him she needed sods for the fire and he said he'd be there in a minute and stopped then at the rasp of footsteps on the gravelled road.

'Off you go now, Tommy', he whispered, his hand in the small of my small back. 'Off you go'.

'He's coming, he's coming!' I cried at the back door and I could feel my heart bigger than my breath and my legs all weak. She let me sit by the cooling range with a cup of milk until my father pushed through the kitchen door after what seemed like forever, a half-filled sack of turf across his back.

'I told him'. That was all he said and I expected more but that was it, though I could hear their whispers long after the lamp was turned down and I lay there, too full of fear to sleep and imagined 'The Bowler' moving in the shadows the branches threw on the windowpane, his eyes glowing, his nails scrabbling, his polished, razored face pressed up hard to the cold, lifeless glass.

Then winter came and with it the winter games of cards. My father sat with a stack of copper coins on the thrumming range, playing 'twenty-five' and drinking tea. They'd sometimes let me play a hand or two, amused at my childish attempts to trump, their voices raised to the low ceiling in excitement when I managed it, explaining how to renege could ruin your game and your good name and watching for my feeble efforts to stifle back the yawns and how one would still creep between my clenched jaws.

'Ah now, young Tommy Walshe', Mack would say. 'Is that Seán O'Noon, the Sleepyhead I see? How did he get in?' And he'd snatch away his hat and scratch at his bald head and laugh.

I hated the Sleep-carrier Seán O'Noon and I hated how he crept between my clenched teeth when I forgot to be watchful. But I was off to bed, touching the stack of heating coins as I passed and knowing that by morning my father would be lucky to have a one or two left and that it wouldn't matter because it wasn't winning that held him but the talk and listen and the sifting news.

I was long asleep and dreaming the night they decided that 'The Bowler' would have to learn. My father had asked him nicely and he'd chosen to ignore it, so now they'd wait further out along the black road and tell him hard.

'When you're the Government you can piss where you like. I know we're bet, but I'll not take that from anyone', was how my father put it.

Years later when she was alone my mother told me how it fell. They were playing cards when the talk came around again and they left the cards face down, the coins stacked, the hands already dealt and went into the black dark beyond the farthest bridge and watched there until he came, whistling, stepping towards the town, nothing in the shadows but the distant lights of Crowley's big house and the army barracks a curving glow across the hill, the Free State soldiers peering into the still, unfriendly dark, the cry of 'Halt' always ready in their dry throats.

She never told me who hit him first but even after all that time she would smile at the thought of the bowler hat and how they'd knocked it from his oiled head and warned him, with words at first and then with punches in his softened, government gut. Harty had lashed out at the hat with his boot and sent it skimming low along the dusty road in the blue moonless dark. 'The Bowler' had tried to rise, groaning that he'd get the police. Then they'd turned on him again, savagely this time and left him battered, crumpled in the road.

They left him there eyeing the dirt with a warning not to come back and Harty had bent and picked the dented bowler and when they reached our house he'd placed it on his head, knocking on our door to scare my mother when she came with his 'good evening ma'am', skipping across the kitchen floor in a nimble dance.

They took turns to try the hat for size and study its foreign shape and place it tentatively on their heads, our kitchen filled with noise. Harty decided it only fitted him, telling the others that they had thick, Irish, potato heads with lumps and how it just wouldn't sit right. Then they smelled the sweet hair oil and noticed how it wasn't new, the hat-band stained with years of sweet pomade, the leather head-band grease stained, the 'size' and 'made-in' signs faded to nothing – the once white triangle on the lining yellowed and decayed.

'Maybe we should have left it?' this from Josie Burke. 'Suppose the 'Free State' police come looking? We'll be guilty as sin'.

What followed then were litanies of suggestions, plans to leave it back, or throw it on the road, or hide it, until finally it was agreed to burn it. They tried to fit it through the top lid of the glowing range but the brim had smouldered and begun to smoke. So they lifted it with a tongs, Harty holding it while Josie and my father struggled with the top metal plate, attempting to slide it aside, smoke belching towards the ceiling and at last Harty eased it to the flames and it began to fry, the hair-oil boiling, clouds pouring from the sweating felt.

'Shut the lid, shut the lid!' Harty exclaimed as I watched, sleep-sodden from my bedroom door, my mother waving her apron at the smoky cloud. But even then the hat wasn't finished and we could hear the hair grease roaring in the chimney breast and what my mother called the moaning whirlwind of the burning hat.

'He'll burn the bloody house!' Harty cried again and we all went and stood in the back garden and watched the flying sparks shooting into the night, some drifting towards the haystacks before rushing back inside to lift the fire out on a shovel into a metal pot, the noxious smoke making our eyes water, the chimney breast already split, shutting the dampers down tight to kill the burning moan. Mack Harty struggled with the shaky ladder, a wraith climbing to the heavens, a wet sack slapping against his thigh and he swung it across the gushing flue, a pepper-shot of sparks flying to the dark.

We stood in the hissing darkness, all eyes on the smoking, puffing chimney before Josie exclaimed, 'the stacks, the stacks', and the ladder was thrown against the nearest one, my father racing aloft, beating at the small wisps of smoke rising from the sides but the dew and the dampness saved us and before long the sparks were out.

When the two policemen came out of the night and asked what was going on I thought that they'd come to help us quench the fire. I remember them taking my father to one side, a firm grip on his arm and talking quietly, pointing towards the road. My father looked plausibly surprised, his hands in his pockets, saying how he had more than enough to be doing here and how his neighbours had been playing cards when the chimney caught and how they'd helped fight the fire.

'Ask them if you like', my father nodded towards Mack and Josie.

The taller of the policeman leant towards my father, poking him firmly on the chest.

'You might think you're smart Walshe, but be careful'.

'Ah, we're all smart now', my father nodded. 'New country, new uniforms, new policemen, new jobs'.

The tall policeman didn't look too happy with that, turning to his partner and nodding in my father's direction. The other policeman came closer, a squat bulk to him and a mean look on his narrow face, a malevolence feeding from him.

'Still as smart as ever, Johnny. How's the brother finding Canada? He got out just in time, didn't he?'

My father said nothing, Mack Harty moving between him and the police. There was something old here, something I didn't understand. Josie stood there too, his fists bunched, saying even less than usual but there was a tightening in the small yard, a cold feeling of something wanting to happen. The policemen felt it too, the taller of the two turning again.

'If he identifies any of you we'll be back. There might be room for the two of you in Canada yet. That's if you make the boat this time'.

The policemen left then, Harty delivering a mock salute as they retrieved their bicycles from the ditch and we stumbled back inside, the house reeking of smoke and soot, all trace of the hat gone, smoke still wisping through the kitchen door. My father went directly to the enamel basin, sloshing water over his blackened hands and it was only then I saw the running traces of blood on his knuckles, the pink trickle of it staining the white enamel as he washed carefully between his strong fingers, Mack and Josie checking their hands as well.

There are gaps in it after that. Like many things remembered it pours out like an old jigsaw, haphazard, some pieces missing, others falling where they may, but I recall my mother looking at me in surprise years later when we finally talked about it and I said the hat was 'The Bowler's' victory because the hat was his revenge.

Look at all we lost: we came to the attention of the new police just after the Civil War and just after my uncle had fled abroad, that war lost. We'd almost burned the house, split the chimney breast, and in some strange way I've never understood it divided good friendships too.

After that night I remember my father being more secretive about things, even if the police never called back. He felt that maybe he had acted rashly, leaving a story out there for others to build on, and giving easy work to anyone who wanted to use it.

At harvest time Josie and Mack still helped and my father returned the work but the cards became less frequent, and then died out. There seemed to be less visiting, as if they looked and saw each other in a new way after that night and what they saw lessened them in some way. 'The Bowler' married in the town, Feeney's sister abandoned in midstream, the whisper feeding out from Feeney's how we were in some way implicated in it all, but it was never said, not to our faces anyway.

About the Author

photo © Joe Geoghegan

James Martyn Joyce is from Galway, where he is a member of The Talking Stick Workshop. His work has appeared in *The Cúirt Journal, West 47, Books Ireland, Crannog, The Sunday Tribune, The Stinging Fly* and *The SHOp*. He has had work broadcast on both RTÉ and BBC and has won the Listowel Writers Week Originals Short Story Competition. He was shortlisted for a Hennessy Award in 2006, for the Francis MacManus Award in 2007 and 2008 and the William Trevor International Short Story Competition in 2007 and 2011. His debut collection of poetry, *Shedding Skin,* was published by Arlen House in 2010.